LP DAR
Darby, Catherine.
Sabre

APR 03 2001   03-18-03 BPL

DATE DUE

**Willimantic Library
Service Center
1216 Main Street
Willimantic, CT 06226**

SABRE

Catherine Darby

Willimantic Library
Service Center
1216 Main Street
Willimantic, CT 06226

Chivers Press
Bath, England
●
Thorndike Press
Thorndike, Maine USA

This Large Print edition is published by Chivers Press, England, and by Thorndike Press, USA.

Published in 2001 in the U.K. by arrangement with the author.

Published in 2001 in the U.S. by arrangement with Robert Hale, Ltd.

U.K. Hardcover ISBN 0–7540–4344–4 (Chivers Large Print)
U.K. Softcover ISBN 0–7540–4345–2 (Camden Large Print)
U.S. Softcover ISBN 0–7862–3029–0 (General Series Edition)

Copyright © Catherine Darby 1985

All rights reserved.

The text of this Large Print edition is unabridged.
Other aspects of the book may vary from the original edition.

Set in 16 pt. New Times Roman.

Printed in Great Britain on acid-free paper.

British Library Cataloguing in Publication Data available

Library of Congress Control Number: 00-092643

PROLOGUE

1817

Buy an Irishman a drink and he'll start telling you how he's descended from one of the kings of Tara. Dadda always said that was like gilding the lily. It was sufficient to be Irish without boasting anything more.

'For 'tis the finest thing in the world to be Irish, Fausty!' he would say.

He not only said it but believed it, and himself with only a few coppers to jingle in the pocket of his threadbare green coat! To be Irish was a privilege conferred by the angels upon certain people who must give due thanks for the honour and try not to look down on other, less fortunate races.

There were times when I could have argued the matter with him, times when I looked around our steamy, untidy kitchen with the broth bubbling over the peat fire and the unglassed windows that let in every draught, and wondered how anyone could possibly consider us fortunate.

'We have a roof over our heads,' said Bridie. Bridie was a year younger than me and fancied herself as an optimist. In that she was different from Dadda who had been born hopeful and didn't need to work at it.

1

'The roof leaks,' I pointed out, 'and the east wind sends all the smoke back down the chimney and the floor's oozing damp.'

'And we're all healthy,' she said primly.

That was true enough but it didn't make things any better. Most local families had two or three babies laid neatly in the graveyard, safely dead and no longer requiring to be fed. Dadda and Mammy had conceived eight healthy children, none of whom had died, and our cabin was practically bursting at the seams with rosy children who never sat still for more than two minutes at a time!

There were eight of us and would have been more if Mammy hadn't died when the twins were born. That had been when I was ten years old and still believed the Holy Mother listened to prayers. I'd prayed on the night the twins were born, prayed for a dead baby and Mammy not able to have any more for ever since I could remember she'd gone about with her stomach swollen and her face small and pinched above. I'd believed my prayers would be answered and, perhaps in a way, they were partly. Mammy never had any more babies because she died when Sean and Stevie were only a few hours old and everybody said we had a new saint in heaven. I wanted a Mammy in the cabin not a saint and from that moment I stopped believing that prayers were heard.

The twins were seven years old now and into mischief every hour. Peg was ten and as wild as they were, forever climbing trees and getting her church shoes scuffed. Mary was twelve and fragile in comparison with the rest though her looks were deceptive for she had never ailed in her life. When she was fourteen she was to enter as a postulant in the Convent of Our Lady of Sorrows and she went about with her rosary dripping from her fingers as if she were practising. After her came Danny, who was thirteen, and as glum as the rest were cheerful. Cathy was a lumpish fourteen-year-old and Bridie was sixteen to my seventeen.

Eight of us and only myself not content to be where we were or even who we were. I wanted to be a lady and, as far as I could see, I hadn't a chance of attaining my ambition as long as I stayed where I was. Real ladies didn't come our way very often, but Dadda had taken me to the Horse Fair at Dublin twice, and I'd seen them there, stepping up into shiny curricles, their hair curled, frilled parasols in their gloved hands, the trains of their narrow skirts draped gracefully over their arms.

One little chance and I was certain that I too would be stepping up to sit on velvet cushions. At seventeen I was pretty. There is no point in denying the fact. I could see it clearly for myself in the ivory-backed mirror that had been Mammy's one little concession to her own vanity. The mirror had come to me after she died and I'd watched myself grow up in it, seeing the round contours of childhood

3

fine down into a heart-shaped countenance. My hair was blue-black and wavy and I had the rosy colouring that country girls have and large, pansy brown eyes with little yellow flecks in them.

'As if one of the blessed angels had blown sunlight into them,' Dadda said sentimentally.

He was always sentimental when he'd taken a drop but any compliment was a pleasure to me. Along with good looks I'd been born with a great craving for admiration. I had dreams in which a handsome gentleman said the most wonderful things to me. Not that I knew any handsome gentleman! The lads roundabout were well enough but I'd sense enough to realise that, if I listened to their blarney, I'd end up in a cabin with a parcel of children all round my skirts. So I kept myself to myself in a way that won the whole-hearted approval of Father O'Brian.

'A modest maid is a jewel in Ireland's crown,' he beamed, his little eyes sweeping me from my braided hair to the hem of my mended skirt. 'Had you any thoughts of going into the religious life?'

'That's for Mary, not me,' I said firmly. 'I'm going to raise the Sullivans up in the world.'

'Are you indeed?' The little eyes twinkled. 'And how do you intend to be setting about such a thing?'

'I shall go to London,' I said. 'To London in England. There's plenty of work there and

4

good wages paid, in gold.'

'I've been hearing that too,' he nodded. 'What kind of work would you be doing in England?'

'I could work in a shop,' I said. 'There are grand opportunities for those who work in the big shops in England.'

'And you speak the English beautifully,' he agreed. I'd taken years to learn how to pronounce the words though none of them have ever sounded as pretty to me as Gaelic. I had been the smartest pupil at the day school that Mrs Flannigan ran. She was an English lady who had wed an Irishman which, it was generally agreed, was the most sensible thing any Englishwoman could do. Her husband was long dead, but she'd stayed on in Ireland, and ran her school for a flat fee of two-pence a week.

'Not that I require the money, my dear children, but anything that costs money is valued more and education is no exception,' she was fond of saying.

Some of her pupils would not have valued what she had to offer if she had charged a sovereign a week, I thought. Most of them considered reading and writing a waste of time. Ladies, however, were always well-educated and, with the goal fixed in my mind, I had applied myself to my lessons with the same fervour that Mary brought to her prayers. After a while, though I never lost sight of the goal, I began to enjoy the lessons for their own sake. Books had a scent of their own unlike anything else and the words in them opened up new worlds for me, places I wanted to visit, experiences I wanted to enjoy. I read all the books that Mrs Flannigan had and I learned to write in copperplate hand that was neater than the priest's. I also took trouble over my needlework, having in mind some idea that I might start my brilliant career by trimming bonnets or making fine lace.

I had ceased full-time lessons three years before but I still went to see Mrs Flannigan two or three times a week. She had relatives in England who sent her the occasional parcel of books which the pair of us devoured and later eagerly discussed. It was so many years since she had been in England that her ideas about the place were as romantically vague as my own and she too was inclined to believe that the streets of London might be paved with gold. One particular afternoon I went over to the small white house, where she lived secluded behind a high hedge, and had not the slightest presentiment as I walked up the flagged path that my whole life was about to change.

Mrs Flannigan was in the front room which was the schoolroom five days out of the seven. This day being Saturday she had covered the blackboard with a velour cloth and pushed the two benches against the wall. I have called it a small house, but I write with hindsight. In comparison with the thatched cabins in which the rest of the village lived, the Flannigan house was spacious. Behind the schoolroom was the kitchen with wooden steps leading up to the bedroom. I'd been sent up there once to fetch something down for her and filled my eyes with the enormous brassbound bed, the flowered china basin and ewer, the fringed rug on the floor. I had never seen anything so luxurious in my life and the realisation that someone could actually have a bed to themselves, not to mention a room, made my head spin.

I tapped on the door and, hearing her bid me enter, wiped the soles of my shoes carefully on the mat spread before the front door and went in. She was at the small desk where she sat during lessons, her spectacles on the end of her nose, a letter in her hand.

'Faustina, you are the very person I was hoping to see.' She gave me the peculiarly sweet smile that was her only charm and gestured to a stool.

Whenever I entered the room I became a schoolgirl again. This afternoon was no different. I sat down meekly, remembering to put my feet neatly together and fold my hands loosely in my lap. It was not such an easy feat because the stool was low and I have always been tall with long legs, but I contrived it and waited patiently for her to continue.

7

'I have received a letter from my cousin, Arabel Whitney,' she said after a few moments. 'I have not seen dear Arabel for many years but she writes to me once in every two or three years. Some time ago I wrote, mentioning you, and enquiring if she knew of a suitable position for an intelligent, attractive young woman.'

'That was very kind of you!' I exclaimed.

'Not at all.' She gave me a faintly reproving look. 'I am always anxious to help any of my former pupils and you have always made it clear that you wished to get on in the world.'

'Oh, I do! I do!' I clasped my hands more tightly together and leaned forward.

'My cousin tells me that she has a place for a young lady companion in her own household,' Mrs Flannigan said. 'She will pay fifteen guineas a year.'

I had never heard of anyone earning so much simply for being a companion. I had never even heard of a companion being paid anything at all.

'She has enclosed your passage money to Liverpool and the fare for the stage to London. It only remains for your father to give his consent.'

'Dadda will,' I said. 'He's always wanted us to get on!'

'As the eldest, perhaps you are expected to remain at home, to care for the younger ones?' she suggested.

'Bridie can do that,' I said quickly. 'She and Cathy are better than I am for keeping the young ones in order, and the money that I send home will make life more comfortable for them all.'

'As long as it is given directly to your sister,' Mrs Flannigan said.

We looked at each other, not saying what we were both thinking. Any extra money that came into the house generally found its way into Dadda's pocket and thence onto the bar counter of the Royal James. He was never one to miss paying his round and, though we none of us ever went hungry on account of his tippling, the fact remained that he was more often tipsy then sober.

'If I sent it to you,' I said at last, 'you could see that Bridie got it, couldn't you?'

'I'd be happy to undertake the commission on your behalf,' she said. 'Now you must return home and discuss the matter thoroughly with your father and with Father O'Brian too. I can reassure him that my cousin, Mistress Whitney, was always a most respectable young lady and will most certainly look after your moral welfare.'

It sounded faintly dull, I thought, but it didn't much matter. Once I had reached London, if I didn't like being a companion, I would look for another post. There were hundreds there, just waiting for eager Irish girls to come along. I was quite convinced of

9

that.

'Will you tell your cousin that I'd be happy to accept the post?' I said politely.

Excitement was bubbling up in me but I had the sense to keep it restrained. Mrs Flannigan was always strict about behaving correctly and I didn't want her to change her mind recommending me to her cousin.

'You must talk with your father first,' she said.

'He'll agree,' I said confidently and rose, bobbing the required curtsey. 'I really am most grateful to you.'

'Not at all.' She waved her hand towards the door in a gesture of dismissal. 'Go along now, Faustina.'

I managed to restrain myself until I closed the gate behind me and then I let out a whoop of joy and danced along, holding my skirts out at each side, and humming under my breath. I realised then that I had never really believed that I ever would actually escape from our crowded, smoky cabin. It had been a dream to hold back the dark and now, quite suddenly, the dream was coming true and I couldn't yet quite believe that it was so.

CHAPTER ONE

Dadda said at once that I could go. He was secretly so much in awe of Mrs Flannigan's great learning that I believed he would have agreed if she'd suggested packing me off to darkest Africa. Having given his consent, he went off to the Royal James and got gloriously and sentimentally drunk, rolling home by starlight with two of his cronies and all of them serenading the entire village. I loved Dadda but there were times when he was an awful trial to me. In England I would be able to think of him with affection without the embarrassment of seeing him so often in his cups.

The younger members of the family reacted to my going according to their natures. Bridie said cheerfully that she would manage splendidly and scarcely notice I wasn't there—there was always something a mite tactless about Bridie. Cathy asked me to send her a present. Daniel reminded me that the crossing to Liverpool was bound to be rough and Mary said sweetly that she would pray for my soul. The others didn't pay much heed to the news. To them England was as far as Heaven.

It seemed an age before I left though it was no more than a few weeks. Mrs Flannigan wrote to her cousin to tell her that I was on my way and Father O'Brian took it into his head to find out the name of the Catholic Church that was nearest to where she lived so that I wouldn't have any excuse for skipping Mass. Others in the neighbourhood either wished me luck or shook their heads sadly reminding me of Brenda O'Grady who died of the typhus three days after she landed.

I was determined not to die of anything. I was equally determined that I was not going to spend the rest of my days as a paid companion. Still in my mind was the handsome gentleman who would ride into my life and snatch me away to happiness.

'You will require a new dress in which to travel,' Mrs Flannigan said.

I gaped at her a little. Surely she realised that money didn't stretch to new dresses in our household! We each of us (the girls I mean) had two bodices and two skirts, a shawl and a pair of shoes, and our clothes were patched, turned, mended, let out and lengthened as we grew. 'I still have some of my trousseau,' she said, smiling slightly. 'We will contrive something with what we find.'

Her trousseau, as she called it, was laid away in lavender in a chest and, for the second time, I went up into her bedroom while she knelt to push back the carved lid and rummage among the garments.

'They are all sadly out of date,' she said, 'for panniers were in fashion then, but the material is still good and the colours not much faded.'

In the end she chose a pink dress with green embroidery on the lower part of the skirt. The bodice had a round neck and little puff sleeves and when all the fullness had been taken out of the skirt she declared it to be very suitable for a young girl. A similar gown of pale lemon, but with long tight sleeves and a higher neck, was also altered to conform with current style, and she was generous enough to supply me with the long cloak of dark green and little matching bonnet that lay, folded in tissue, at the bottom of the trunk. For the rest she produced a quantity of white lawn which I sewed into shifts and drawers and two nightgowns. It was the first time in my life I'd had even one nightgown! There were even two pairs of shoes, Mrs Flannigan having the same sized feet as my own, and three pairs of knitted stockings.

As each garment was altered and completed and packed into the corded trunk my feelings of anticipation grew. I had sense enough to realise that handsome gentlemen were more likely to notice even the prettiest of girls if she was becomingly clad, and I was quite determined to be noticed by a handsome gentleman. A handsome *rich* gentleman, I amended, and turned with renewed interest to polishing the buckles on the almost unworn shoes I had acquired.

We were to drive the ten miles or so to

Dublin in Father O'Brian's rig. At the last moment as I climbed up beside him and looked down at them all standing there, I felt an immense sadness as if a gulf had already opened between us. Early that morning I'd gone to Mass and then, back to Mrs Flannigan's house where she'd filled a tub with hot water and produced soap and towels. I was a mite nervous about catching a terrible chill with stripping off my clothes in April, but she had her schoolmistress face on and I didn't dare argue. Now, in the yellow dress and the dark cloak, my hair tied back under the little bonnet, I knew that I looked very much like the young lady I hoped to become, and though I was eager for the adventure to begin there was a grief in knowing that I was already separate from them.

'You have the address safe?' Dadda said, coming to the side of the rig.

'And my tickets,' I assured him. He was sober, it being early in the morning, but there was a look in his eyes that told me he would probably be very drunk by the end of the day.

'And the money? You have the money safe?'

I had two sovereigns to buy food along the way. We were to have an overnight stop at a place called Derby and Mrs Flannigan had already written ahead to reserve me a bed. I'm afraid that at the time I was inclined to take much of her kindness for granted, but I can see now that she went to a great deal of trouble on my behalf. I think that she hoped that one of her pupils would do well in the world and so reflect credit on her teaching.

'I have everything safe, Dadda,' I said.

'You be a good girl now and minding your manners and be writing home,' he said.

There was a mist of tears in my eyes and I wanted to jump down and hug him fiercely and tell him that I'd always be his Fausty, his girl, but Father O'Brian was clicking his tongue to the two ponies and there was no more time. I looked back once as we bowled along the dusty track and saw him gazing after me, his green coat flapping, a smile clamped to his face, and he already seemed an immeasurable distance off.

I had been to Dublin before but then I had been a child, clinging to Dadda's hand or lifted on his shoulder to watch the horses parade. It was still a crowded, noisy place, however, with tall buildings and a bewildering number of people. Father O'Brian knew the way to the docks which was fortunate as, left to myself, I'd have been hopelessly lost in five minutes. As it was it took him some considerable time to locate the right boat and then the rig had to be left in charge of a boy while the Father shouldered my small trunk and escorted me up a creaking gangplank to the canopied chair in the secondclass section to which my ticket entitled me.

There were some very grand people with

English accents on the deck above and I saw many more people being herded below, the women with shawls over their heads, others with their luggage tied up in a bundle. They were travelling free as ballast and at Liverpool would get on a boat bound for America whose streets were even more thickly paved with gold than those in London.

'There's food here,' Father O'Brian said, putting my trunk at my feet, 'and a little flask of the poteen to keep out the cold. You'll not be talking to any strangers now!'

I couldn't see how I was to leave home and not talk to any strangers but I mumbled something.

'Remember to let us know as soon as you're settled and don't be picking up any flighty English habits,' he instructed. 'Be a good girl and say your prayers and do your best to turn your back on temptation.'

Poor Father O'Brian! The good man had no idea that the demure young girl to whom he spoke was determined to run and embrace any temptation that came along. He made the sign of the cross over me and went down to the wharf again where he stood, patiently waving, as the gangplank was withdrawn and the great vessel shuddered into life.

Contrary to Dan's prognostications the crossing was a smooth one but I think, even if it had been rough, I would have been too interested in everything that went on to feel sick. The sea was so much bigger than I'd imagined and it wasn't blue at all but a greenish-grey with white lace edging the waves. Above us the great sails billowed out and, if I tilted my head, I could see men, small as fleas, climbing the rigging. All around me people were settling themselves, some in chairs lashed to the deck such as I occupied, others leaning over the rail or strolling up and down. I could hear all the accents of Ireland in the mixture of English and Gaelic being spoken, the mellifluous lilt of Tipperary, the harsher sounds of Cork, even the hard, Scots twang of Ulster. I was far too nervous to leave my trunk unattended and so remained in my place, eating the cold tatie cakes that Father O'Brian had given me, and taking sips of the poteen as the sun sank and the night wind blew more keenly. I was warm enough in my thick cloak and, though I'd expected to stay awake, I drifted off to sleep, lulled by the movement of the boat and the sounds of the sea. I woke with a jerk, sunshine beating on my closed lids, the smell of tar and salt in my nostrils. I sat up straight, reaching to make certain my trunk was still in place, and strained my eyes towards the approaching shoreline. I would have liked leisure in which to savour my first stepping on to English soil but the passengers were rushing to the rail to point out various landmarks and the pigtailed sailors were shinning up the masts and tossing mooring ropes to the stone quay.

My impression of Liverpool was of a bigger, noisier Dublin. The wharf was crammed with boats and there were huge, grey sheds and towering warehouses blocking the skyline. I looked about me in confusion having been jostled along the gangplank, carrying my trunk awkwardly in both hands. I am a tall, well-built girl but standing on the quay, I felt suddenly small and vulnerable.

'Cab, Miss?' An exceedingly grubby boy had popped up at my elbow and was giving me an inviting, gaptooth grin.

'I have to take the stage for London,' I told him.

'You'll be wanting the coaching yard, Miss.' He relieved me of my trunk lifting it easily despite his scrawniness and led me between bales of stuff being unloaded down a twisting alley to a yard-which gave on to a posting station where a team was being hitched. I gave him a penny out of the coppers in my purse and he touched his forelock, the first time that had ever happened to me, and yelled up to the coach driver in his high, nasal voice:

'Lady for London!'

'Inside or outside, Miss?' The coachman heaved my trunk to the roof.

'Inside.' I showed him my ticket and he nodded briskly.

'Starts in about half an hour. If you're just off the boat you can get a wash and brush up

18

and a bite to eat in there.'

He jerked his head towards a narrow door with a painted sign swinging above. I entered, trying to look as confident as if I'd been walking in and out of public places all my life, and found myself in a very respectable hostelry where I was able to make a decent toilet and buy a steak pie and a mug of porter.

When I took my seat in a corner of the coach I felt completely refreshed and was looking forward immensely to the rest of my journey. Holy Mary and all the saints! but I must have been as green as grass not to realise how uncomfortable it would be squashed in a stuffy carriage that was jolted up hill and down dale at a speed that fairly terrified me. There was a leather strap hanging at the side of the window and I clutched it with whitened knuckles as we bowled along. There were actually people sitting on top and I was in mortal fear that one of them would fall off and be killed, but they must have been too wicked to die.

The other people who sat inside with me were English, I knew that, not only from the few words they let drop, but from their general stiffness of manner.

'The English are not friendly to strangers,' Dadda had told me once. 'They keep themselves to themselves.'

They were not even friendly to one another, I decided. At home we'd not have dreamed of going two miles in company with another without settling to a good gossip about his family and his crops and the disposition of his landlord. Here they merely nodded coolly, barely parting their lips to smile, and murmured that it was warm for the time of year. My own wide smile and cordial 'good morning' was met with an embarrassed shuffling of feet and a few muttered replies. I thought at the time it was because I was Irish, but I know now that if I'd have carried a written guarantee of pure English blood their reaction would have been just the same.

I occupied myself with looking out of the window but for most of the time we went at such a speed that hedges, trees and houses rushed into a blur, and after a while I closed my eyes and concentrated on keeping my seat without being flung into the lap of the portly gentleman who sat opposite. We had a short stop at midday and then we were off again, jolting towards Derby. The towns all looked much the same to me and the countryside was somehow small and cramped with a haze of smoke lying between roof tops and sky. Everybody in England had begun to burn coal as well as wood and the smoke from coal is black and sticky and smells bad, unlike peat which has a sweet scent and cooks more evenly too, in my opinion.

By the time we reached the coaching inn I ached in every muscle and my legs felt weak as water. One of the other ladies in the stage was complaining of feeling sick but I had discovered myself to be of a strong stomach and so was spared that indignity.

The inn was large and, to my eyes at least, very comfortable, though the next morning I heard another of the passengers grumble that his mattress had been too hard. For my own part I could have stretched out on bare boards and not noticed! I was so tired that it was an effort to eat the plentiful supper provided and I was asleep the moment my head touched the pillow. I rather regretted that for it was the first time in my life I'd had a bed of my own in a room of my own. The room was only the slip of a chamber under the eaves and the bed was very narrow, but I would have liked to have stayed awake long enough to enjoy the privacy.

Breakfast was another substantial meal. The English, I was beginning to discover, were great trenchermen. I would have liked to linger over the ham and eggs and so delay the moment when I had to climb back into that wretched coach, but the driver was keen to be off again. I found out later that the various stagecoach companies held wagers as to which could cover the distances in the shortest time.

To my surprise I found myself more attuned to the motion than on the previous day and to my further surprise, one or two of my fellow passengers acknowledged my greeting with frosty little bows. I settled myself in my place

21

and, though my limbs still ached, began to enjoy the journey more though I still wished the stage wouldn't tilt so alarmingly when we went round the corners. I noticed too that whenever we crossed a stretch of commonland there were uneasy glances exchanged and the portly gentleman folded up his newspaper and brought out a pistol, observing as he caught my eye fixed on it in alarm.

'If any footpads show their noses, ma'am, I intend to give them a fight for it!'

To my relief no highwaymen appeared, and before dusk fell we were driving at a more sedate pace through cobbled streets with high buildings at each side that shut out the light. London had stolen upon me unawares and I gazed eagerly out of the window, trying to see as much as possible before the darkness became too intense. The streets were crowded with people even though it was near evening and several flaring torches were lit at the corners of the buildings. We turned into a wide thoroughfare and drew to a halt. An instant later the coachman appeared at the door.

'Young lady for Wadcome Park Square?' he enquired loudly.

'That's me!' I accepted his help down the high step and saw that my trunk was already on the pavement.

'Straight down that road and you'll come to it,' he advised me.

'Thank you, sir,' I wondered if he expected

a gratuity but he was already clambering up to his seat again, and I stepped back hastily as he urged his sweating team onwards.

It took me a moment to get my balance after so many hours in the swaying coach and then I picked up my trunk, there being no obliging small boy to volunteer his services, and made my way down the short street the coachman had pointed out into the square with its halfmoon of handsome houses. It looked very grand, like the big houses in Dublin where the genteel ladies and gentlemen lived. Dadda had shown them to me when we went to the Horse Fair.

I wanted number 25 and it was easy enough to find, for all the numbers were printed in gold letters on the newel posts. There were lamps hanging over the fanlights of the front doors and the houses had railings running along the outsides of them. I think I would have stood there for hours staring up at the handsome facade but the door opened suddenly and I was confronted by the first completely black human being I'd ever seen.

He was small and coal black with thick lips and a broad nose and the whitest teeth I ever saw. His clothes were so grand that I wondered if he were a prince or something. His coat was of white brocade and embroidered with gold, his breeches white satin, and on his head was a scarlet turban. He flashed the white teeth at me and said in a soft, deep voice with a queer sing-song accent.

'Missus says that you are to come right on up and not stand agaping there.'

It was an odd sort of invitation and he obviously wasn't a prince for he darted down the steps and picked up my trunk and then he led the way up into a narrow hall and down the passage into a square, panelled room with what seemed to me a very large number of mirrors. I could see myself reflected every time I turned my head and became quite fascinated by the varying views of my profile.

'So this is my cousin's protégé!'

The remark came from an elegantly dressed lady with a fluff of yellow curls on top of her head. She was as different from Mrs Flannigan as it's possible to be, but there was the same charm in her smile. She was reclining on a couch and I thought at first that she must be an invalid for I'd never heard of anyone lying down in the daytime before. Later I was to discover that Arabel Whitney was completely idle and almost completely selfish. I say 'almost' because her selfishness was shot with unexpected gleams of kindness. It had been kind of her to ask Mrs Flannigan to recommend a companion and now that I had arrived that same kindness led her to give me a cordial reception.

'Take off your cloak and bonnet and sit down,' she commanded now. 'Sambo shall bring us some coffee, and when we've talked you shall have a tray in your room. What a pretty creature you are! You put me in mind of myself at your age, save that I was always blonde.'

I didn't think there was the least resemblance but I murmured something polite as I took off my garments and sat down on a straight-backed chair with a velvet cushion. Sambo, who had vanished somewhere, returned with a tray on which were two cups of coffee in china so thin one could practically see through it.

'Such a journey as you must have had!' Mrs Whitney said, sipping her coffee with a languid air which I'd never succeed in imitating. 'You must be dreadfully fatigued!'

'I'm feeling better by the minute,' I said cheerfully.

I'd only drunk coffee once or twice before and, to tell the truth, I prefer a dish of black tea or a tot of poteen. However I sipped away manfully while Mrs Whitney went on gazing at me as if she were learning me by heart.

'And how is my dear Georgina?' she asked finally. That must be Mrs Flannigan. I had never heard her Christian name before.

'She's very well,' I assured her.

'We used to be very intimate friends when we were girls,' she said. 'That was before either of us was married. Poor Georgina was never a belle, I fear, but she was always very clever. Most clever, which is not always

25

admired by the gentlemen but Mr Flannigan admired her very greatly. Such a pity that she was widowed after so short a time! My own dear husband died only five years ago and I have never considered remarriage though I must tell you that I have not lacked for offers.'

She paused to put down the cup on a small table near to her hand and patted her froth of curls. She looked much younger than Mrs Flannigan, her figure slight, her skin powdered and carefully rouged.

'I am sure you have not,' I said politely, but it really wasn't necessary for me to say anything at all. Arabel Whitney was one of those people who don't require anything except a dumbly admiring audience.

'We were most beautifully contented together,' she went on, patting her hair again. 'Mr Whitney said to me very often that he blessed the day he ever married me! Wasn't that a charming thing to say! And since his death I have kept the entire house as he would have wished it to be.'

'It's a lovely house,' I said, meaning it sincerely.

'Mr Whitney always had exquisite taste.' She took out a minute handkerchief and dabbed her eyes. The lids were painted a pale blue that matched the colour of her eyes and the loose draperies she wore.

'Mrs Flannigan said you were wanting a companion,' I said.

'Someone to see to accounts, plan menus, make those domestic decisions that are so tedious,' she said vaguely. 'A little sewing from time to time. The gentlemen like to see a pretty face about the house.'

'Gentlemen?' I must have looked slightly aghast for she gave a tinkling laugh and said 'My dear Faustina—such a quaint name by the way—Mr Whitney made his living from Lady Luck, if you catch my meaning.'

'No, ma'am,' I said frankly.

'Mr Whitney kept a salon, my dear,' she explained. 'Gentlemen of the quality come here three or four evenings a week to play whist and faro. It is pleasant for gentlemen to have somewhere quiet and comfortable where they may enjoy a little flutter.'

'Oh,' I said blankly.

'I like to think that we have a most exclusive clientèle,' she was continuing. 'At one time or another the noblest feet in Britain have crossed the threshold of this house.'

'Does Mrs Flannigan—?'

'My cousin is a lady and naturally never enquired into the source of my late husband's income,' Mrs Whitney said with a faintly reproving air.

'Oh,' I said again.

'Now you must see your room.' She rang a tiny silver handbell and the black boy came in again. 'Tonight you may eat in your room but when my health permits I do enjoy company at

27

dinner.'

'Yes, ma'am.' Recognising the signal to depart, I rose, dropped her a curtsey, and followed Sambo out of the room and up two flights of stairs into a square landing off which various doors opened.

'In here, Miss.' He opened one of the doors with something of a flourish and ushered me into a very pretty room. There was a carpet covering the entire floor and the walls were not painted but hung with a striped cream and blue paper. There were blue curtains at the window and my trunk stood at the foot of a blue quilted bed.

'Your dinner's here, Miss.' Sambo darted to a covered tray on a table in the window and lifted the lid. 'Anything else you just ring for it.'

'Is your name really Sambo?' I asked curiously.

'No,'m.' His grin split his face from ear to ear. 'But all us black boys is called Sambo. Saves Miz Whitney from having to think.'

'Are there more of you?' I enquired.

'Three of us in this house, Miss. Most ladies only have one so it's a feather in her cap. She got us as a present from her husband when he visited Liverpool. We do all the work in the place, 'cepting the cooking.'

'And it is really a gambling den?' I lowered my voice as I spoke but he answered in the same cheerful tone.

'A salon, ma'am. Cards, dice and

champagne. Very select. Miz Whitney keeps it on in memory of her husband. Very happy together they were.'

'I see. Thank you.'

'Anything you want you ring,' he repeated and went out.

The dinner—at home, we'd have called it supper—was a feast. There was a cold, pale green soup which I learned to recognise later as asparagus, boiled tongue and a salad, and peaches sprinkled with brown sugar. I ate heartily, aware that the tiredness in my limbs was seeping away and that I was beginning to enjoy my new situation.

Mrs Flannigan would be horrified if I wrote and told her that her cousin ran a gambling den. The poor lady imagined her relative to be a widow living in only slightly better circumstances than herself. And Father O'Brian would insist that I went home on the very next boat before I slid further down the slope to perdition and then I would be trapped for ever in our, smoky, draughty cabin.

I decided that I wouldn't mention anything to Mrs Flannigan. There was, after all, no point in worrying everybody unnecessarily. It wasn't as if I'd be gambling myself.

There were more lanterns lit in the square below for it was quite dark by this time. I rose from the table and went to the window to pull the curtains across. From where I stood I could see a couple of small coaches standing, their drivers chatting together as they leaned against the railings. A flood of light shone out down the short flight of steps that led from the house I was in and two gentlemen, walking across the square, went up the steps and disappeared from view within the porch. I drew the curtains and knelt to unpack my trunk. There was still time for me to tell Mrs Whitney that I'd changed my mind and wanted to go home again. She would probably be greatly put out after all the trouble she had taken but I was not so timid that I couldn't face a little unpleasantness. Failing that I could write to Mrs Flannigan and then Father O'Brian would make sure I went home even if I had to swim the Irish Sea.

Of course I knew very well that I would do neither of these things. The dinner had been too delicious, the room too pretty, my welcome too friendly. The truth was that I'd caught the scent of money and social advancement and I wasn't about to give it up. I went on unpacking my clothes, putting them away in the big carved wardrobe and the chest of drawers. Last of all I put Mammy's ivory-backed mirror on the dressing table. It was both a link with my past and, when I looked into it, a promise for the future.

CHAPTER TWO

For all the vice I found at Number 25, Wadcome Park Square, Father O'Brian could have come and stayed and been as unshocked as if he'd been staying in a monastery. For the truth was that Arabel Whitney was as respectable as Mrs Flannigan believed and her gambling salon was run as strictly as a school. Only in the evenings were the two large drawing rooms on the first floor opened up and clean decks of cards set out on the round baize-covered tables. The rooms were very handsomely appointed, decorated in shades of nutmeg brown, cream and gold. There were deep armchairs with wide arms on which glasses and ashtrays could be conveniently balanced and a rack in which journals and newspapers were arranged. The lamps were hung so that the surface of those tables in use were brightly illuminated. I had always imagined that a gambling den would be a place where no decent person would ever come, but the gentlemen who came to Mrs Whitney's salon were not only respectable but well born. Nobility even! They were smartly dressed, their cravats intricately tied, their boots polished until one could see one's face in the gleaming leather. They spoke in the slow, drawling accents of fashionable London and at first I was so much in awe of them that I scarcely dared to open my mouth in their presence, but I hadn't been many days at the house before I realised that under their fine manners they were not much different from Dadda or any of the other men in our village. Those who hadn't wives were generally hoping to be married and those who had wives tried to escape from them as often as possible. They wagered high stakes, higher than I could have believed possible, and I never got over my awe at seeing such sums of money regularly won and lost.

During the play the Sambo who was on duty would come round with glasses of Madeira and champagne and thin, sugary biscuits, and once or twice during the evening Mrs Whitney would drift through the rooms, pausing to smile at one, to exchange a few words with another, her draperies fluttering.

At first she took me with her, introducing me as 'Miss Faustina, my young visitor from Ireland.' It sounded rather grand though I think they all realised from the beginning that I was employed there, especially as she was in the habit of referring to Sambo as 'my young visitor from Africa.' But my duties were so light that there were times when I made belief that I was the daughter of the house. Mr and Mrs Whitney had never had any family which, in my view, was a blessing for she would never have coped with a squalling baby. In many ways she was a bit like a child herself, for she liked to be fed and amused at regular intervals, and she was apt to sulk when she found herself neglected.

'When Mr Whitney was alive we often mingled in the best society,' she said wistfully. 'We went to the opera, my dear, and to Vauxhall Gardens, though not on Saturday nights, when the demi-monde frequented. After Waterloo there were displays of fireworks. Most elegant!'

I liked to hear her talk. I even tried to imitate her accent and the way she had of moving her thin white fingers to emphasise a point. I never succeeded, of course. Ireland was too strong in me. But I do flatter myself that I began to move more gracefully and that my voice became less outlandish in pitch and pronunciation.

After a while, if Mrs Whitney was having one of her frequent naps, I used to go up to the salon by myself to watch the gentlemen wagering. There was no noisy calling of the odds such as I'd seen at local pony races and cockfights. There was only the murmur of a wellbred voice, a rustle as a note of hand was slipped across the table.

Then, one evening, after I'd been there about six weeks it changed. That was the evening I met Earl Sabre and the moment I laid eyes on him I knew that everything that had happened to me up to that instant no longer counted. I noticed him, partly because I had not seen him at the gambling tables before, and partly because he was the type of man who would be noticed in any company.

He was tall. I am tall myself but he topped me by a good head and he was broad across the shoulders with long legs encased in immaculate breeches. His hair was red which we in Ireland regard as a misfortune because Judas had red hair, but it was not carroty or even that strawberry-fair shade that passes for red. It was dark russet, lying against his well-shaped head in deep waves, and his eyes turning towards me as I entered with Mrs Whitney were a cold, clear grey fringed with long reddish lashes which might have been considered girlish had his features not been so decidedly masculine.

They say that love at first sight is only an illusion and they may be right. All I know is that when it happened to me it was more real than anything else I had ever experienced. I stood, drinking in every detail of him, and then he bowed slightly and Mrs Whitney rustled towards him with as much animation as I had ever seen her display.

'My dear Sabre, I had no idea that you were in town!' she exclaimed.

'For a while, Mrs Arabel.' He kissed the tips of her fingers and looked past her as he straightened up to where I stood. 'And if you were ten years older, my dear lady,' he continued, 'I would swear that you had been hiding a daughter from all your friends!'

'No relative at all, my dear Sabre,' she returned flutteringly. 'Faustina Sullivan is staying with me on an extended visit.'

'Sullivan?' He bowed over my hand, his cool grey gaze still lifted to my face. 'You must be from Ireland. I have never visited there though I am always promising myself that I will go one day. My good friend Charles assures me the hunting is first rate.'

I had sufficient wit left to smile and bob a curtsey though my heart was hammering under the thin pink stuff of my bodice. I was used to the admiring glances from the lads at home and several of the men who came to play cards here had paid me compliments, but this long, searching look was something I had not known before, and I was too young to deal with it.

'It's a long time since we had the pleasure of your company, Sabre,' Mrs Whitney said.

'I've been up north to see my family.' He was still looking at me and I could feel the colour rising into my face, spreading over my neck and chest.

'And they are all well, I trust?' Mrs Whitney enquired.

'Well enough.' There was a faint wryness in his voice that made me look at him in puzzlement. 'They were glad enough to see the back of me.'

'I'm sure you exaggerate!' She tapped him

playfully on the arm and drifted away.

I don't think that she expected me to follow her but, even if she'd given me an order, I don't believe I could have moved a step. I was rooted to the spot, swallowed up in that cool, grey gaze.

'And will you know me when we meet again?' the newcomer asked softly.

'I don't know you yet, sir.' I pulled myself together to answer him boldly. 'You know my name and I have heard only one of yours.'

'For which piece of ill manners I should be soundly chastised! I am Earl Sabre, Miss Sullivan.'

'A real earl!' I couldn't help exclaiming, and he laughed, throwing back his head to display blunt white teeth.

'I'm sorry to disappoint you,' he said at last, 'but Earl is my Christian name.'

'I never heard it before,' I confessed.

'It was my grandfather's choice. He was exceedingly miffed when the king didn't see fit to reward him with even a simple knighthood for the many services he considered he had rendered the Crown and insisted that his eldest grandson should bear the name of Earl. I prefer to use my surname so I trust that you will oblige me by doing the same.'

'If you wish.' I hesitated and added, emboldened further by his friendly manner, 'My name is Faustina, after the blessed martyr, but I am generally called Fausty.'

'Fausty from Ireland.' He bowed again, grey eyes no longer cool but dancing. 'Will you drink a glass of champagne with me, Miss Fausty, before I take a hand in the game?'

'I don't like champagne,' I said frankly, 'but I'll watch you drink a glass, if you like.'

'Splendid.' He touched my arm, steering me to a small sofa in the window bay, taking a glass from Sambo's tray as we passed.

I sat down, glad to do so because my knees were still shaking, and he sat down beside me, stretching out his long legs in their tight breeches and gleaming boots. He was not a fop. His cravat was tied neatly but not in the elaborate style that made it hard for some gentlemen to turn their heads, and the only jewellery he wore was an engraved onyx ring.

'From what part of Ireland do you come?' he enquired.

'A village just outside Dublin, sir.'

'Not 'sir', but 'Sabre'.' He touched my hand briefly, his fingers burning through to the marrow of my bones. 'It's a long way from Dublin to London.'

'In more ways than one,' I agreed fervently. 'But my schoolteacher was a friend of Mrs Whitney's when they were both girls. I'm here as a sort of companion.'

'Fortunate Mrs Whitney!' He raised his glass to me and drank.

'She's been very kind to me,' I said.

'I've no doubt. Arabel's not a bad sort.' He

spoke carelessly, his eyes still on my face.

'And you're from up north?' I began.

'Yorkshire.' The wryness was in his voice again. 'My family lives up there.'

'But you don't?'

'I visit,' he said briefly. 'However moorland and mill can grow wondrous tiresome after a while so I keep apartments down here and escape whenever I can.'

'Oh, that was how I felt when I was at home,' I said, delighted that we had something in common. 'I love my family, of course, but the cabin was so poky and I wanted to make something of myself.'

'You appear to have succeeded.'

His eyes strayed to the low neckline of my bodice and I felt the queer, bubbling excitement rise up in me again.

'Shouldn't you be playing?' I felt a little stab of guilt at keeping him from the tables.

Rather to my disappointment he set down the glass and rose, smiling down at me.

'You ride, I take it?' he enquired.

'I've ridden ponies at home, but not properly, with a saddle,' I told him.

'Then you must allow me to teach you. I'll call round tomorrow afternoon.'

He didn't ask me if I wanted to go. I think he knew already that nothing on earth would have kept me at home.

He bowed and moved away, greeting a couple of gentlemen who made room for him at their table, and I went on sitting in the window bay until I was sufficiently in control of my own limbs to walk out of the room.

I was not sure how to set about asking leave to go riding but the next morning Mrs Whitney told me there was a riding habit of hers that would probably fit me.

'I've not ridden for nearly ten years,' she said with that air of wistfulness that made it sound she would give anything to be able to take an invigorating gallop somewhere. 'I was plumper in those days, so the jacket won't be too tight.'

'You don't mind my going out?' Up to then I'd been dutifully to Mass and I'd taken a stroll in the railed green park that gave the square its name, but I hadn't ventured further.

'With Earl Sabre? He asked me leave to take you riding. A young girl needs a little amusement.'

'Do you know him well?' I wanted very much to talk about him but wasn't certain how to begin.

'He plays here sometimes. An old Yorkshire family. Very good blood there, I believe, but he doesn't get on very well with his father.'

She spoke vaguely, leaning back against her cushions and closing her eyes. I suppose that the effort of finding a habit for me had brought on a fit of nervous exhaustion. I was glad that I was young and full of energy and I ran upstairs briskly with the outfit she had given me over my arm.

The skirt was too short for I was taller than she was and the jacket was a trifle tight across the shoulders but the dark blue suited my black hair and rosy skin and I put one of my own cotton bodices underneath and, in lieu of a hat, tied a scarf over my head.

It was past three before he came and I had been ready for ages, tweaking my skirt into place, arranging my scarf in a more becoming manner, deciding that, at the last moment, he must have regretted the impulse that had led him to invite me. Then Sambo tapped on the door to tell me that the gentleman was come and I forgot all the resolutions I had made about behaving in a calm, English manner and ran downstairs, my skirt flying out above my ankles.

'Good day, Fausty from Ireland.' He had dismounted, doffing his hat, looking even taller and handsomer than I remembered from our brief interview of the previous evening.

'Good day to you.' My smile was wide and welcoming, though I shot the two horses an uneasy glance. I'd hared about on the little half-wild ponies that grazed near our village but these were sleek riding horses, one with a side-saddle that looked very uncomfortable.

'She's accustomed to young ladies,' Sabre said, intercepting the glance. 'Or so the stable man assured me. We'll go at a sedate walking pace so all you need to do is to hold on and

40

accustom yourself to the feel of the saddle.'

'I've always ridden astride,' I told him.

'If you were to ride astride here you'd scandalise half London,' he said teasingly and lifted me up to the saddle as easily as if I were a feather.

It was easier than I had feared. The skirt of the habit was split so that I could hook one leg over the pommel as he instructed and, as we walked across the square through the gates that led into the park, I found the gentle motion quite pleasant.

'You have good hands and a good seat,' Sabre approved. 'Next time we'll try some trotting.'

So there was to be a next time. I gripped the reins and tried to sit as proud and straight as any English lady. He had not asked me if I wanted to go, but I suppose he already guessed how I felt.

We didn't talk very much. I was too intent on staying on and sitting correctly and Sabre seemed content to amble along in my wake. There were flowers in the park, not spilling wild out of the hedgerows as they did at home, but standing in banked rows with iron railings round them. Living in London was a bit like that, I thought, and a wave of homesickness rippled through me as strong as the breeze that had sprung up.

'Couldn't we try trotting now?' I pleaded.

'If you like.' He reached, a sudden spark of

mischief in his eyes, and slapped my mount on the rump.

A second later and I was careering down the gravelled path, the saddle slipping, my fingers tangling desperately in the horse's mane. Sabre couldn't have expected such a result for I heard his exclamation of alarm and then trees and fenced flowers were racing past me and the sky was tilting sideways. I had the sense to kick my foot free of the stirrup and then I was flying through the air. I landed, praise the saints! on a bank of soft grass and lay, winded, staring up at the blue sky across which fleecy clouds were drifting.

I became aware that someone was stooping over me. Not Sabre but another man, clad in equally elegant riding clothes, his broad face puckered up in concern.

'Are you all right, Miss?' His voice was sharp with worry.

'I think so.' I sat up cautiously, gasping slightly. Sabre had just dismounted and was striding towards me, concern and amusement in his face.

'That was my fault! I didn't know your mare had such a skittish streak,' he began and broke off, extending his hand to the other gentleman. 'Chas! Chas O'Hara! What the devil are you doing in town?' he demanded.

'Amusing myself. How are you, Sabre?'

'Amusing myself,' Sabre retorted and the two of them clapped each other on the back.

'I could have been killed,' I said with as much dignity as I could summon up from where I sat.

'You fell like a star from heaven,' the man called Chas said, offering me his hand.

I struggled to my feet, smoothing down my skirt. The fall had loosened my scarf and my hair streamed loose over my shoulders. Both men were looking at me with open admiration, and I was conscious, amid my confusion, of a feeling of power. It was not that I was interested in the newcomer. He was shorter than Sabre with wide shoulders that looked out of proportion in contrast to his thin legs, and his broad face was freckled. But it was pleasant to have two pairs of eyes resting on me with such frank appreciation.

'Miss Fausty, may I present my good friend, Charles O'Hara?' Sabre said, remembering his manners with effort. 'Chas, this is Miss Faustina Sullivan from Dublin.'

'Surely you are from Ireland too, Mr O'Hara,' I said.

'My grandfather was, but I've never laid eyes on the place, though I'm beginning to regret it,' he answered.

He meant to be pleasant, but his gallantry was heavyhanded and his eyes were set too close. However he was Sabre's friend and I was eager to like whatever Sabre liked.

'Sabre's a sly dog, keeping you to himself,' he said taking my hand again.

'I only met the young lady myself yesterday,' Sabre protested. 'She's staying at Arabel's for a time.'

'Is she now?' Chas O'Hara's eyes swept over me again. 'If I'd known Arabel had such pretty relatives I'd be throwing the dice more frequently.'

'Chas may never have set foot in Ireland,' Sabre remarked, 'but he got hold of a piece of the blarney stone!'

'Shall we mount up again?' I asked, not wanting to be rude but hoping the threesome we had become would split up again. I had been enjoying the lesson.

'Are you sure you're not hurt?' Sabre enquired.

'I want to get back in the saddle,' I said. 'Isn't that what you're suppose to do when you've had a fall?'

'The young lady has pluck,' Chas O'Hara said. 'You ought to take better care of your conquests, Sabre! She might have broken her neck or been spiked on one of those rails.'

That was exactly what I had been thinking but I was irritated by his criticism of Sabre. The other merely laughed and lifted me back to the saddle, hands firm at each side of my waist.

'I hope I may have the pleasure of calling on you, Miss Sullivan,' Chas O'Hara said. 'To satisfy myself that you're not hurt.'

I didn't want him to call on me at all but it

would have been impolite to say so. I smiled with what I hoped was the right degree of frostiness and he stood, hat in hand, watching Sabre remount and turn the horses.

'Who was your friend?' I asked as we turned down another path.

'Chas? Oh, he's a younger son of a younger son,' Sabre said. 'Not two farthings to rub together but a good sport.'

'He talked too smoothly,' I said.

'Ah, that's just his way.' Sabre flashed me a smile that was hurtful in its lack of jealousy. 'He's quite a one for the ladies is old Chas! Do you still want to learn how to trot?'

'Not your way,' I said, 'but if I could take off this foolish saddle I'd show you a tearing Irish gallop!'

'Tell me about Ireland.' We had left the formal park and emerged on to a small piece of common dotted with beech trees, and the sunlight dappled his hair with gold.

'There's too much to tell,' I said. 'I could never explain it. The countryside isn't neat and pretty like this. It rolls all around you like the sea and there's a fine mist over everything. But when the sun shines then everything glitters as if it's been turned to gold and even the squealing of the pigs has a happier sound.'

'You've a touch of the blarney yourself, Fausty Sullivan!' He dismounted and lifted me down, leading both horses across the grass to where a stream bubbled between the trees. I

45

walked at his side, secretly relieved to be on my own two feet again.

The horses bent their heads to drink from the stream and Sabre rolled up his cloak into a cushion and set it under a beech tree for me.

'England is the land of opportunity though,' I said, taking the improvised seat. 'Anyone who wants to get on in the world must come to England.'

'Is that what you want, to get on in the world?' He had dropped to the ground beside me and his grey eyes were amused as they rested on my face.

'Surely, doesn't everyone?' I exclaimed.

'My father would applaud your sentiments,' he remarked. 'Getting on is his substitute for a creed.'

'My father never had any ambitions for himself,' I admitted, 'but he'd never stand in his children's light.'

'You've brothers and sisters then?' His hand moved to cover my hand, his fingers stroking the inside of my wrists in a way that sent little shivers up my spine.

'Too many,' I said feelingly. 'Oh, it's not that I don't love them all, but they're forever under my feet! Bridie, she's next in age to me, is nearly grown up but the others are all young. My mother died when the youngest were born, so Bridie and I helped rear them.'

'Is that why you want to get on in the world?' His voice was low, interested, and he'd

46

moved closer, his other hand pushing the scarf from my head. 'For the sake of your family?'

'For my sake too,' I was honest enough to admit. 'I got awfully tired of peat and pigs.'

'Fausty of Ireland,' Sabre said, 'you are a lovely, lovely creature!'

I wanted to say something to him that would express my own feelings. I wanted to tell him that in all my seventeen years, I'd never known such emotions as those that coursed through me now. I had not dared to hope that he might have been struck by those same feelings, but it was clear that he had been because there was a look in his grey eyes that mirrored the desires surging up in me, and he was pressing me down into the sweet grass, his hand tugging up my skirt, his mouth crushing into silence all the things I'd wanted to say.

I could make excuses. I could say, quite truthfully, that in Ireland young people frequently leapt the broom before they could get round to having the banns called. Most folk turned a blind eye to such doings and, provided the wedding followed shortly afterwards, not much was ever said. I could tell you that this was the most beautiful man I had ever seen and the first time I had ever been so private with any man.

The truth is that I thought up the excuses later. At that moment I had nothing in me but a consuming hunger to hold and to be held, to feel his mouth on mine, his hands stripping the tight jacket from my shoulders, slipping beneath my bodice to hold the waiting globes of my breasts.

I shiver now to think how easily we might have been seen. The city of London was all about us and on a sunny afternoon almost anyone might have strolled into the green space where we lay, but by some miracle we had it to ourselves and nobody came.

Afterwards, when the soft moans of loving were stilled and our garments straightened, I found a comb tucked into a pocket of the skirt and combed my hair. There were bits of grass in it and Sabre laughed, taking the comb from me and tugging it through the tangles.

'Lord, but you have lovely hair!' he said. 'Like black silk it is and your skin like a rose! And I was your first?' His voice held a wondering note.

'Of course you were.' I felt hurt that he should ever consider there might have been others, and he laughed again, dropping the comb and pressing his hands at each side of my face.

'Of course I was,' he said and kissed me, first on one cheek, then on the other. There was such a very great tenderness in him. I wasn't mistaken about that.

'I love you,' I heard myself say and he smiled, releasing me, his eyes warm as he answered, 'I love you too, Fausty of Ireland! Now I'd better lead you back to Mrs Whitney's or people may start guessing what we've been doing.'

I thought they would probably guess anyway once we'd arranged the wedding, but he was helping me to my feet, and shaking out his cloak, and then he lifted me to the saddle, and we were leaving the green space behind as we entered the well-regulated park again.

'Will you ride with me again?' he asked turning his head as we approached the gates.

I gave him a look of blank surprise. The English had peculiar customs and no mistake if a man had to enquire if the girl he loved wanted to see him again.

'I'll ride with you tomorrow,' I said.

'Not tomorrow, sweetheart.' He shook his head regretfully, 'I'm meeting some friends at White's, but I'll probably drop by a day later. I lost some money last night and I want to recoup it. The day after will be entirely yours. What would you like to do?'

'Make love,' I said promptly, and he burst out laughing.

'My darling, I adore women who have no false coyness,' he said at last, 'and we shall certainly make love again, but there must be places of interest you'd like to see. London's the greatest city in the world!'

I wanted only to be with him, not wandering round looking at places of interest, but then I realised if Sabre ever came to Ireland I'd want to show him the grand houses in Dublin.

'I'd like to see the Tower of London,' I said, thinking back to history lessons with Mrs Flannigan. 'And Westminster Abbey. They let people in those places, don't they?'

'Even Irish girls with black silk hair and brown velvet eyes,' he said gravely, but his eyes were dancing. I was glad that I amused him, but I couldn't help feeling that he was taking what had happened between us very lightly. By this time an Irishman would have been demanding the right to speak to my father. In England they evidently went about things in a different way.

We had reached the house and Sambo was holding the door open. Sabre dismounted and helped me down but though I put up my face to be kissed, he bent and kissed my fingers instead.

'I'll call upon you in a day or two,' he said softly.

No doubt gentlemen didn't kiss their sweethearts in public, so I submitted with a good grace to the coolness of the embrace and went up the steps into the narrow hall.

It was odd but I didn't feel very much changed. I was happy, happier than I had been in my life, but apart from a little stiffness—and that was due as much to the tumble I'd taken as anything else—apart from that, I felt exactly the same as when I'd set out, and when I looked in the mirror there was only a wisp of grass in my hair to remind me that anything had ever happened at all.

CHAPTER THREE

'I hope you will come riding with me one morning,' Chas O'Hara said.

He had called upon me for the third time in a week and, to tell the truth, I was heartily sick of him. Oh, he was the soul of politeness! He sat at least two yards away, drinking the negus that Sambo brought in, making what the English call small talk. Most of it was about himself. For a man who didn't have two farthings to rub together he was full of his own importance. He had been sent down from Oxford for gambling, had made the Grand Tour, and now lived in bachelor quarters, partly on a tiny allowance allowed him by his long-suffering father and partly by his wits. He told me about his successes at faro and dice, about the wagers he laid on horses and cocks, about the sports in which he took part.

'Rowing is a splendid way of developing the muscles, Miss Fausty,' he said earnestly. 'But boxing beats all! I fight at light heavy-weight— that's the term we use.'

'Oh, indeed?' I turned a yawn into a smile and wished that Sabre would come. He came only once or twice a week and though almost a month had passed we had not had the opportunity of making love again. That was because Chas O'Hara, either by chance or design, always turned up about five minutes after Sabre did and the three of us generally sat talking or ended up by walking out together, Sabre on one side and Chas on the other. Any other girl might have been flattered by having two gentlemen dancing attendance on her, but I wanted to be alone with Sabre. I was falling deeper and deeper in love with him and I wanted time to talk about our future together. But Chas was always there and Sabre never hinted by word or look that his presence was unwelcome. It was almost as bad as having the twins round my feet, I thought gloomily.

'So if you would give it your consideration,' Chas said.

'I beg your pardon?' I jumped slightly as I realised that he was talking to me.

'I wouldn't expect an answer at once because my prospects aren't brilliant, but my father would gladly increase my allowance if I gave him assurance that I intended to settle down.'

'Oh, I'm sure that he would,' I said.

'But Sabre tells me that he doesn't believe you to be indifferent to me,' Chas said.

Something inside my head rang a loud, warning bell and I could feel my eyes widen as I stared at him.

'My taking an Irish bride would please my father too because of our own descent,' he continued. 'I wish that you would give me an answer soon.'

'Oh, I will,' I said blankly.

'In three days?' To my horror he reached out and grabbed my hand, kneading it between his own so hard that I winced. 'I have to go out of town for a little while but I'll be back by Saturday. I wouldn't go out at all but I've a long standing engagement to race my curricle to Bath and there are wagers laid on me.'

'I hope you win,' I said.

'Oh, I think I will!' He gave my hand a final punishing squeeze and, to my relief, dropped it. 'My greys are well matched and deep in the chest. Good staying power. But I'll be back on Saturday and then—oh, Miss Fausty, I shall eagerly await your answer!'

I sat there too embarrassed to say a word, and God forgive me! but the only hope I had was that he might break his neck in the curricle race. I'm ashamed of that, but this is a truthful record.

He must have thought that I was overwhelmed by the honour he was paying me or mistook my blank horror for bliss. He rose, smiling all over his broad, freckled face, bowed and went leaving me in what must have been a mild state of shock because it was a full five minutes before I could collect myself sufficiently to ring for Sambo to remove the tray.

It would have been comical if it hadn't been

so dreadful. To imagine that my being pleasant to him, because he was Sabre's friend, meant anything more simply proved how foolish he was. The most awful part of it was that he had actually said that Sabre thought I wasn't indifferent. Either Sabre had been in his cups when he said it or he too had misunderstood my politeness for encouragement. I was in a fever for the evening to come and for Sabre to call.

I was never more relieved to see him and praise the saints! Chas O'Hara had not accompanied him. I'd been half-afraid he might have changed his mind and come back. As it was Sabre kissed my fingertips and went immediately to one of the gaming tables, not noticing my frantic signals. It was more than an hour before he rose and sauntered over to where I sat fidgeting by the door, and by that time I was almost of the opinion that he was as stupid as his friend.

'Pretty Fausty!' He spoke softly, his grey eyes warm on my face. 'Forgive me for neglecting you, but I had promised Twist a game—unfortunate name for a gamester!'

'Sabre, I need to talk to you,' I broke in. 'Not here but somewhere private.'

'I've something to tell you too.' He offered me his arm and we moved out to the landing. There was a small sitting room just beyond the head of the stairs and I opened the door, picking up a lamp from the window sill as I went in, for the chamber was unlit.

'It must be important,' Sabre said, amused. 'This is certainly private enough!'

'Nobody comes here very often.' I put the lamp on the table and went into his arms, clinging to him in the way I had wanted to for a month.

'Is something wrong?' he asked, holding me away to look into my face.

'Chas O'Hara came here today and asked me to wed him,' I blurted out.

'Did he now? I thought he'd get round to it sooner or later,' Sabre said with interest.

'You mean you knew he was going to ask me?'

'He hinted that he might. What did you say?'

'I didn't say anything. I was too surprised.'

'I'd take him if I were you,' Sabre said. 'He's no fortune, but his family's well connected, and it's time old Chas settled down.'

For a moment I was sure I hadn't heard him properly. It was some kind of jest between them to test the strength of my feelings for him. It had to be a jest. I swallowed because there was suddenly a lump in my throat, and said.

'But you and me? What of you and me?'

'Darling Fausty, I love you dearly,' he began, but I shook my head and took another step away from him.

'Don't say that unless you mean it,' I said

55

sharply. 'I thought you loved me! After what—'

'Sweetheart, I'm devoted to you,' he said, but it was all changed, all wrong. The warmth in his eyes was for any girl with whom he happened to be and his lovemaking had been no more to him than a half-hour's pleasure to while away an afternoon.

'I thought you wanted to wed me.' My voice was small and thin and the lump in my throat was grown so big that I felt as if it were choking me.

'I'd like nothing better,' he returned, not meaning it. 'But I'm not the marrying kind of man, Fausty. Don't you think my father hasn't said the same thing to me over and over, reminding me that I'm his only child and the name dies with me unless I take a wife?'

'Well, here you are then,' I said weakly.

'Sweetheart, when my father tells me to take a wife,' Sabre declared, 'he means a young lady from the district, or even a London girl.'

'I thought you went your own way and didn't care what your family thought.'

'Up to a point I do, but I've got the sense to know how far I can go before I get cut off without a penny to my name.'

'You could work,' I said, but he shook his head, amusement in his voice as if he were talking to a child.

'I'm not trained to earn a living. Oh, my father taught me sufficient about the mill to enable me to distinguish one end of a loom

56

from another but he wanted me to lead the life of a gentleman. He wouldn't be very amused if I—'

'Married beneath you?' I burst out as my voice returned. 'That's what you're going to say, isn't it?'

'It's what my father would say. If I were completely my own master it would be different.'

'You're twenty-five years old! You told me so yourself? Do you have to wait until you're fifty before you cut the apron strings?'

'I lead my own life, but I'm not such a fool as to risk losing a fortune by wedding a girl my family wouldn't accept.'

'They don't even know me!'

'Fausty, you're Irish and a Catholic. That would be sufficient. The Sabres have been High Anglicans since Tudor times and the only Irish they ever heard about were navvies working on the roads and a few weavers who were brought over to work the new frames when we had the Luddite trouble.'

'I never built a road or worked a loom in my life!' I cried in fury. 'I'm as well educated as any prinking English Miss! And you led me to believe we were going to be married.'

'Now be fair,' he interrupted. 'I never mentioned marriage.'

'You said that you loved me!'

'I do love you, Fausty. I love you very much.'

'Then it's the same thing,' I began.

'No, Fausty. No, it's not the same thing.' He seized my hands and his eyes no longer danced, but were serious and steady. 'I do love you, Fausty, but in my world people don't marry for love. Dear God, but I could have offered to set you up as my mistress. I had more concern for you than that.'

'So you handed me on to your friend! Did you tell him that we'd—?'

'Don't be so foolish! As far as Chas is concerned you're as pure as the Virgin Mary and if you get him drunk enough on the wedding night he'll never know differently.'

'That's coarse!' I tore my hands free.

'Don't forget that I didn't have to force you to flip up your skirts,' he said.

'I love you. I'd fallen in love with you!'

'And I've just told you that love doesn't have anything to do with getting married.'

'Chas O'Hara's in love with me *and* he wants to marry me!' I said triumphantly.

'That's probably his Irish blood,' Sabre said.

My own boiled over at that. There was nothing but a red haze before my eyes and I struck out wildly and heard myself cursing in Gaelic more fluently than my father ever did even when his horse came in last in a race.

'Fausty! Fausty, stop it!' Sabre had caught me by the shoulders and was shaking me.

My vision cleared but the anger was still bubbling inside me.

'I'm not going to change my mind because

you fly into a tantrum,' he said and shook me again to emphasise his point. 'I do love you, Fausty, but there's no way I could ever make you my wife and expect my father to understand. Chas will be a good husband and his family won't object as much as mine would. I came here tonight to tell you that I'm going up north for a while. When I come back—'

'I hope you never come back,' I said, and my eyes were dry and burning as if my anger had scorched all my tears. 'I hope you stay up north and marry an evil-tempered wife and that all your children are born naked and you lose all your fortune—and your father—' I paused, partly because I was out of breath and partly because I couldn't think of anything bad enough to wish on his father, and while I hesitated he let go of me so abruptly that I almost fell over, and walked out, slamming the door behind him.

I was all alone in the neat little room with the lamp burning bright as my anger on the table and all the pride and passion draining out of me. God be my witness but I've never been one who couldn't, in the end, recognise the truth and the truth was that I'd been a fool from the start. I'd left Ireland full of grand notions about raising myself in the world and the only thing I'd raised was my skirt, spreading my legs like a Dublin trollop for the first man who came along. I'd fallen into his hands like a ripe peach and it made no difference that I had loved him at sight, that I truly believed he would marry me. I blamed myself bitterly for being a fool and I blamed him more for taking advantage of the fact.

He had probably left the house but I didn't go back to the gambling salon to see. Instead I went up to my own room and pulled off my dress with shaking fingers. There was water in the basin, still lukewarm, and I seized a sponge and began to wash myself all over as if I were trying to make myself the way I had been before. It wasn't any use though I scrubbed myself red and even poured a jug of water over my hair. It wasn't any use because you can never wash away the touch of the first man who takes you.

The next morning I woke with such a queer, heavy feeling in my head, as if some dreadful thing hung over me. I wondered if having my heart broken had given me second sight. There was a woman I'd heard about in Galway who could read the future after her husband was drowned in a sea gale. But I felt sick too and when Sambo came in with the usual cup of chocolate the smell of it made me retch. That was when I realised that my monthly curse was late, at least ten days as far as I could reckon.

I sat up in bed, frantically counting on my fingers. It wasn't possible! Everybody knew that nothing could happen after the first time. But it had happened to me. I couldn't wash it away any more than I could wash away the memory of Sabre's touch.

For a few minutes I came very close to despair. Oh, I know despair is a sin, but I was already a sinner and one more wouldn't make much difference to me. There was nothing I could do and nowhere I could turn. I thought of finding out where Sabre lodged—he had never mentioned exactly where it was, but one of the gentlemen who played here every night might know. And then what? He had probably already left for the north and I'd no way of reaching him there. Even if I did I had the horrible suspicion that he wouldn't consider a child sufficient reason for marriage. The most he would probably do was to pay for its support.

There were places where a girl could go. I'd heard whispers from a few of the older women in our village. But it was a worse sin to murder an unborn child than it was to conceive one and anyway the girls themselves often died in agony. I didn't want to die in any manner. I wanted to live and get even with Earl Sabre who'd taken me for a fool.

Something inside me went hard and cold, and the feeling of dread that hung over me lifted. This was the last time, I vowed, that I would let events shape me. In future I would be the one to shape events, and the first thing I must do is to get myself wed as speedily as possible and provide my child with a father. I remembered then, with a thrill of alarm, that I had wished a broken neck on Chas O'Hara. As soon as I was dressed, and the queasiness in my stomach had gone, I went round the corner to the church. There were not many Catholics in London so I was lucky to have a church so near. Mass was finished, but I went in anyway and lit two candles, one for Chas and one for the babe inside me, and still I hadn't wept. At that time I didn't think I would be able to weep again.

Chas O'Hara came back on Saturday and my resolution to take him almost faltered when I was confronted by the reality of his freckled face and the spindly legs under the wide torso. I could never imagine myself growing to love him. Then I reminded myself that I was in England now where marriage had nothing to do with love.

'Did you win your wager?' I asked him politely.

'By half a mile!' His voice was jubilant. 'I'm in funds now, so my allowance will stretch further over the next six months.'

'That's nice,' I said vaguely.

'Miss Fausty, when I last came I asked you a question,' he said. 'I wondered if you'd thought about it, come to any decision?'

'The answer's yes,' I said. I spoke abruptly because it's better to get unpleasant things over quickly.

'You will marry me?' He looked surprised. Perhaps English girls were more hesitant when they accepted proposals.

'Yes. Yes, I will.'

He had flushed with pleasure and, for a moment, I feared he was going to kiss me, but he contented himself with gripping my hands while he spoke jerkily, words bubbling out of him in short spurts.

'My dear Fausty—may I call you so now that we are to be wed? I am more happy than I can say! We must have Sabre as our groomsman.'

'No!' I drew my hands away sharply and the word shot out like a bullet.

'I thought you'd like Sabre.' Chas looked slightly hurt. 'After all you met him before you met me.'

'Only the day before. He's gone up north anyway.'

'Does that mean that you'd agree to a short engagement?' he asked eagerly.

'I would like to be married as soon as possible,' I said. 'I don't want to delay.'

'Won't we require your father's consent?'

It would take time, I calculated, to send word to Ireland and Dadda might take it into his head to come over and inspect the bridegroom for himself.

'My father has always trusted my judgement,' I said. 'Mrs Whitney is more like my guardian now, and she will be happy to see me comfortably settled.' I hoped that was true. She was far too lazy to be a demanding mistress, but I had an uneasy feeling that I had not even begun to earn my promised fifteen guineas. 'What of your father? Will we need his consent?' I asked.

'My father will be relieved that I've decided to settle down,' Chas said. 'He's forever saying that I need a wife to steady me.'

'Will we live at your family home?' I asked.

'Not if I can help it,' he grinned. 'My mother's a darling but she's apt to fuss. My elder brother and his wife live near them out in Hampshire and Frank would certainly come to the wedding.'

'He could act as your groomsman,' I suggested.

'That's a splendid idea.' Chas looked pleased. 'I can see you're going to be a marvellous help to me. I never was the cleverest fellow in the world!'

'I think we'll get along very well,' I said brightly—too brightly because I needed to convince myself more than I needed to convince him.

'Oh, we will indeed!' This time he did kiss me but, at the last moment, I averted my face and his lips only brushed my cheek.

'I think it would be better to—to wait,' I said and hoped that he hadn't sensed my instinctive withdrawal, but he seemed to take my coyness as the natural behaviour of a young lady who had just promised to marry him.

'I will speak to Mrs Whitney at once, with your permission,' he said, kissing my cheek at once. 'And we must discuss the wedding. Our being both Catholics will simplify matters. If we post the banns at once we could be married in three weeks. Would that be too soon?'

I had hoped that it might be sooner, but the child would have to be a seven months' child. I forced a smile instead and said that I would be happy to be married in three weeks and endured another squeeze of the hand before he went off in search of Mrs Whitney.

So I was engaged! I didn't know how I felt about that. I was trying to crush down my real emotions because I knew that this was the only way I could go through with this marriage.

Mrs Whitney sent for me in a little while. She was reclining as usual on the couch in her flower-decorated parlour and, as I entered, she patted her fluff of fair hair and shot me an unexpectedly shrewd glance.

'Mr O'Hara tells me that he wishes to marry you,' she said. 'I must say I am pleased that you succeeded in catching a husband. Every young lady ought to be wed, though not everyone has the good fortune to find a man like the late Mr Whitney. But it means I shall have to find a new companion, or perhaps another Sambo? It is so fatiguing to have to make up my mind.'

'I'm sorry if it's inconvenient,' I said, hoping she wasn't going to ask me to have a longer engagement.

'Oh, I don't much mind.' She waved a

languid hand. 'I do feel rather pleased with myself that I should have set you in the way of matrimony. Not that the O'Haras have any money, my dear. They have a small place somewhere in Hampshire but Charles prefers to live in town. He's something of a sporting man, you know. Most tiring but we must make allowances for the masculine sex. They have a great need for violent exercise. Will your family come over for the wedding?'

'I don't think so, though they'll be pleased to hear about it,' I said.

'You will require someone to give you away, my dear,' she said. 'I believe that a female may fulfil that office so I shall be most happy to undertake that duty.'

Such an offer from the indolent Arabel Whitney represented, I knew, a considerable sacrifice. I thanked her warmly and in a flush of generosity she promptly offered to give me double the salary she had promised me as a dowry and buy me a wedding gown.

'As it is to be a quiet occasion I would suggest something you can wear later when you entertain guests,' she said. 'A pale blue linen with one of the new white bonnets in military style would be pretty and suitable for a June wedding.'

'That would be lovely,' I said.

'And we shall have Cook bake a cake for the breakfast.' She was becoming quite animated at the prospect of a little gaiety.

'This is very kind of you,' I said, glad that at least I could be grateful to her even if I could feel nothing.

'You must write to your family and I will write to Georgina Flannigan,' she said. 'I shall tell her that you have made a most suitable match and that I am sorry to be losing your services so soon. Some of my other gentlemen clients were very taken with you.'

I excused myself, fearing that she might mention Sabre, and went upstairs to write to my father. I would tell him that I was marrying a pleasant young gentleman, Catholic and of Irish descent—that would please Dadda. I would tell him there was no point in a long engagement because we were both certain of our own minds and June was a fashionable month for English weddings. I would write to Mrs Flannigan too and send her ten guineas out of the thirty that were my dowry.

There would be fittings for the new dress, and the priest to tell and flowers to choose. I was going to be mercifully busy during the next three weeks and at the end of it all I would walk up the aisle to be married to Charles O'Hara. Only two things could possibly save me. Earl Sabre might have a change of heart and come back to ask me to be his wife, but I couldn't believe, even in my moments of wildest hope, that he would change his mind, or it was possible that my curse would come late and, as day followed day, I knew that wasn't going to happen.

CHAPTER FOUR

In Ireland a wedding was almost as noisy as a wake. The poteen flowed like water and Sean who played the fiddle like an angel made the music. There were bells hung on the donkeys, and a pig slaughtered to provide a feast for all the guests, and dancing that went on until the stars paled. But that was in Ireland. In England everything was circumspect and in very good taste, but I'll wager even those who wanted to get married didn't enjoy themselves half so well.

My new dress of pale blue was piped in white, the brief bodice having a melon-sleeved jacket cut away at the high waistline to reveal the stylish narrow skirt. My hair was coiled at the back of my head and the tiny white hat with a blue feather curling about the brim perched on top. I carried a posy of white rosebuds and nobody in the world could have guessed how thoroughly and completely miserable I was. The pearl and garnet ring that Chas had given me had been transferred to my right hand for the ceremony and Mrs Whitney, in a burst of generosity, had presented me with a pair of pearl earrings. Pearls for tears, I thought, but I had not yet wept.

I had received a letter from Mrs Flannigan written in the flowing copperplate she had tried to teach all her pupils.

'My dear Faustina,

'Your letter reached us safely and we are all delighted to learn your news. I must confess to a feeling of almost maternal pride in your betrothal and forthcoming nuptials. I had hoped that you might make a good marriage and, from what my dear friend, Arabel, tells me of Mr Charles O'Hara I am convinced your choice of husband is a wise one. I do wish both of you every happiness for the future.

'The money you sent was most generous, particularly in view of the commitments you must have at this time. I will consult with Bridget as to the wisest method of spending it. She has taken over the duty of caring for the younger children with great strength of purpose and Catherine is proving a great help to her. The rest of your brothers and sisters are all well, though I regret to say the twins have already played truant from school twice since your departure. It is a very great pity that they cannot see the advantages of a sound education.

'Your father wishes me to write on his behalf giving his formal consent to your marriage and expresses the hope that you and your husband will honour us with a visit before very long.

'Your sincere friend, 'G. Flannigan.'

I doubted very much if Dadda had used that turn of phrase, but the sentiments were his. I wished he had written himself but he never was much of a hand with a pen.

We drove the short distance to the church in a handsome gig with Sambo perched up behind us. Mrs Whitney had donned a pelisse trimmed with sealskin which looked rather too warm for the day and all the way there she kept patting my hand as if I were going to have a tooth drawn.

There were a few people in the church, some being friends of Chas, others having come in out of the heat of the day to sit down. There were flowers on the altar, and a priest waiting, and a gentleman standing up with Chas and looking so very much like him that I guessed he was Francis O'Hara.

When one is truly miserable everything gets blurred around the edges. It was a mercy because I think if I'd seen everything clearly then I would never have gone through with it, and all I can remember now is that the rosebuds were wilting and my new shoes pinched.

After the ceremony the priest shook hands with us and then Mrs Whitney and I got back into the gig and drove home with Chas and the other guests following on horseback.

There was champagne and an iced white cake decorated with shamrocks, because of the Irish connections, I suppose, and if Sabre had been the bridegroom I would have enjoyed it very much. But I dared not think of Sabre.

'I must say we are frightfully pleased that Chas has decided to settle down,' his brother said, coming up to me and shaking my hand all over again. 'My wife would have come but she's soon to be confined.'

'Con—oh!' I realised what he meant.

'Our fourth in five years,' he nodded. 'This time we're hoping for a girl. Not that my boys aren't jolly little fellows but one likes a daughter. Sybil would like a daughter.'

'I hope she has a safe confinement,' I said and thought wryly that very soon she would be wishing me the same.

I had not thought past the wedding breakfast. I'd deliberately closed my mind to the fact that I had promised to spend the rest of my life with a man whom I didn't even like very much and it gave me a nasty, cold little feeling when Chas touched my arm and said, 'It's time for us to be leaving.'

'Leaving?' I don't know why but I stood there quite prepared to argue.

'On our honeymoon trip, dear. Frank has paid for us to have a fortnight in Brighton. It's our wedding gift from the family.'

'That's very generous of them,' I said.

'Glad to do it, m'dear,' Frank put in.

'Your trunk is packed,' Mrs Whitney said.

For a wonder she had stayed on her feet for the entire reception and was now beginning to wilt slightly. I had the impression that she wanted to wave us off as swiftly as possible so that she could sink down on to the couch again.

We were to drive to Brighton in a hired coach. I was glad of that because I had no desire to have Chas drive us at a boastfully spanking pace along the narrow roads. What I hadn't realised was that the moment we were closed into the coach he would lunge at me and kiss me so roughly that my hat nearly flew off. I grabbed it with one hand and fended him off with the other, my voice stuttering with indignation.

'What in the name of God do you think you're doing!'

'We're wed now,' he said.

'Holy Mother! Not five minutes married and you're all over me!' I said crossly. 'Do be keeping your distance and let me be catching my breath!'

'You're shy.' Chas sat back in his corner and gave me a tolerant look that made me want to hit him.

'Frank told me that Sybil was just the same, but now she's about to be confined for the fourth time.'

'I'm sorry,' I said. 'You must give me a little time.'

'Yes, of course.' He spoke kindly but there was disappointment in his face. After a moment he began to point out various landmarks through the windows and the journey became more tolerable.

It was late when we arrived and the only thing I wanted to do was to fall into bed and sleep, but Chas was with me and I knew he would expect something more. We had apartments at a handsome hotel with a sitting room of our own as well as a bedroom. I took one look at the velvet-draped bed and hastily suggested that it would be pleasant to have a meal.

'It's ordered!' he said with an air of triumph. 'Salmon and roast duckling, a couple of capons, sweetbreads—how does that sound?'

'Indigestible,' I said wryly.

'You'll be in a mood for eating when you've recovered from the jolting of the carriage,' Chas said. 'I've ordered a couple of bottles of port too.'

I remembered Sabre's advice. 'Get him drunk enough on the wedding night.'

'Some wine would be pleasant,' I said brightly, and watched him hurry out to call the waiter. There was a bell-rope by the fireplace but he hadn't noticed it. It was the first indication he'd given of being nervous. That ought to have softened me towards him, I know, but I didn't want Chas as a bridegroom at all.

Mrs Flannigan had a number of sayings which she produced at appropriate occasions. 'What cannot be cured must be endured', was one of them. I applied it firmly to my own situation and, when Chas returned, I was smiling.

The meal was good, if a trifle heavy, but I was too busy filling up Chas's glass to appreciate any of the courses properly. I half-feared that he would prove to have a hard head for liquor but, to my relief, by the time the first bottle of port was nearly empty he was already beginning to slur his words. I drank two or three glasses of the stuff myself and by the time the lamps had been lit and the quilt turned back my head was spinning. I struggled out of my dress with some difficulty for it hooked down the back and I didn't want Chas to help me and by the time he weaved his way in from the outer sitting-room I was between the sheets in one of the high-necked nightgowns I'd brought with me from Ireland.

I would have given much for the gift of forgetfulness that night. If I had never known Sabre I think I could have borne my bridegroom's hurtful fumbling, his wine-sodden breath and mumbled endearments. As it was I dared not struggled for fear of hurting the child and I certainly had no inclination to respond, so lay miserably tense while the marriage was consummated after a fashion. Not until Chas was snoring at the other side of the bed did the long-pent tears come, and even then I feared to weep aloud lest he hear me and I be tempted to blurt out the truth.

We stayed two weeks in Brighton. Before two days had passed Chas had discovered the gaming rooms, as well as a couple of old acquaintances, and for much of the time I was spared his company. My morning sickness had diminished and I took long walks, not in the fashionable streets but along the beach where the sun glinted on the white sands and those who ventured into the water emerged from the bathing machines and bobbed up and down at the end of long ropes. It was supposed to be a healthy exercise. For myself I'd sooner have remained unhealthy!

I was glad when our honeymoon was over and we returned to London. At least I could set up housekeeping properly and I had no doubt that Chas would quickly return to his old pastimes and so leave me free to do what I wanted to do. The trouble was that I didn't know what I wanted to do except to wake up and find that I was Fausty Sullivan again instead of Mrs Charles O'Hara.

Our apartments were on the first floor of a large house near Lincoln's Inn Fields in a pleasant part of the great sprawling city. There was a young lawyer and his bride occupying the rooms below us, and a French lady, who claimed to have been a countess before the Revolution drove her from Paris.

The rooms were big with high, moulded ceilings and the dark heavy furniture of an earlier age. There was a strip of garden at the back where a mulberry tree grew, spreading its branches against the wall, and beyond that a maze of cobbled alleys and stone arches which gave on to trim green lawns.

'Who pays for this?' I enquired, when we had settled in.

My clothes hung in the wardrobe and the first meal I'd cooked for my husband bubbled in a pot over the kitchen fire. Chas, lounging in a chair, answered carelessly.

'My father pays the rent and when I married he increased my allowance, so we won't starve.'

'But you're a grown man,' I said uneasily. 'You cannot expect to live on your father's bounty for ever!'

'Frank will inherit the estate and the bulk of whatever my father leaves,' he told me. 'When my father does die Frank will continue the allowance. He's a good fellow so you need have no misgivings.'

'Most people work for a living,' I frowned, 'unless they're terribly rich, and your father's estate is very small, isn't it?'

'Oh, I increased my allowance,' he said, 'by all sorts of ways. I've been lucky in my wagers these past few months and then there are the rowing and the boxing.'

'That's not a profession,' I put in.

'I've no taste for anything else,' Chas said, yawning and stretching his arms behind his head. 'I did think once of going in for the Law, but there are so many books to be read. It made my blood run cold just to think of all that learning! Then there's the Army, but I fancied being killed even less than I wanted to wear out my brain with studying.'

'You ought to do something,' I said, but he reached up lazily, pulling me down to his knee and nuzzling my ear.

'I'm perfectly content to devote my time to you,' he said. 'We're newly married and nobody expects me to rush off and earn a living.'

I pulled away from him, all my cross and disappointed feelings rising up in me as I said, 'And nobody expects you to sit at your ease either, getting under my feet! Do let me loose! I've the meal to get.'

'I thought it was cooking.'

'Probably burning by now! Chas, let me go!'

I pulled myself free at last and retreated a few steps, straightening my gown.

Chas, looking up at me, said in an aggrieved tone, 'You're damned cold, Fausty! Every time I go about to touch you you sheer off!'

'I don't like to be mauled about,' I said.

'But I'm your husband and a husband has rights.'

'Which you exercise.' I spoke coldly disliking the whine in his voice. I was fast reaching the stage when I was beginning to dislike everything about him. I disliked his lank fair hair and his freckles and his spindly legs, though he couldn't help any of them, and though his company irritated me I resented the fact that he had the right to wander off to see his gaming friends and leave me alone.

The supper was not, after all, burned, but Chas, still smarting from my rejection, shook his head to a second helping.

'Stewed beef and potatoes is a pretty dull dish,' he complained.

'It's what we had in Ireland, and generally without the beef,' I said sharply.

'We're not in Ireland now.' He shot me a disagreeable look. 'You'll have to cook more varied dishes or else we'll be forced to eat out all the time. I did in my bachelor days but a married man expects to come home to a better supper.'

'If you want oysters and goose,' I said, 'you'll have to give me more money to buy them and to employ a cook! I never learned how to make such things!'

'My allowance doesn't stretch to a full-time servant.'

'Then find some employment and increase it!'

'By God, but you nag like an Irish shrew,' he muttered and, reaching for his hat and cloak, flung out, leaving me with the dishes to scrape and water to boil for the washing of them.

I decided that I had better buy a cookery book and learn how to make something more than stew. At home we had eaten mainly potatoes and cabbages with an occasional shank of bacon or rabbit in it. Chas would certainly be justified in expecting more, and a guilty little stab pierced me as I admitted to myself that if I had loved Chas I would have slaved for hours to prepare him the most delicious meal I could devise.

I washed the dishes and went downstairs to sit for a while under the mulberry tree in the garden. There were times when I felt confined by the walls of the city and irritated by the neatly-laid-out parks. It was so different from Ireland where the countryside spread itself all around, even intruding into the streets of Dublin so that wild flowers grew up freely between the cobblestones and the houses in summer were wreathed in creeper.

It was cool under the tree and the lilac twilight was stealing across the grass. The younger lawyer sat in the window of the downstairs apartment, his head bent over his books. I could see his shadow on the net curtain and then a smaller shadow glided up behind him, leaning to embrace him, and the lawyer forgot his books as the two shadows met and merged.

I averted my eyes, feeling as if I were intruding on a little piece of private happiness, and saw the elderly Frenchwoman coming through the gate that led into the pleached alley beyond. She had introduced herself on the first hour of our arrival with a graciousness designed to make us appreciate her condescension in deigning to speak to such humble folk as ourselves. Now she bowed her head slightly as I made room for her on the bench.

'Good-evening, Madame la Comtesse.' I smiled, unconsciously holding myself straighter.

'Madame O'Hara.' She inclined her head a second time. 'It is a delightful evening, is it not? At this time of year London is almost bearable, I think.'

'I was thinking of Ireland,' I said bluntly.

'Ah, yes! You are a native of that country, are you not?' She tapped her silver-headed cane on the flagstones. 'I have never visited there.'

'It's a beautiful land,' I said fervently. 'The air is soft and the rain falls so gently, and the peat fires send blue perfumed smoke up into the sky.'

'It is Paris of which I think,' the countess said. 'Of lilacs and the chestnut trees along the boulevards. I could not endure to go back. So many of the people I knew when I was a girl lost their lives in the Terror. Now you still have a family, have you not, and can visit your country when you choose?'

'I suppose so.' I thought of our crowded,

smoky cabin where the younger children slept in a tangle of arms and legs. Chas would hate it and despise me and though I didn't love him I had sufficient pride left not to want him to look down on me.

'You are alone,' the countess said.

'My husband went out for the evening,' I told her.

'Leaving you here to dream of Ireland.' Her heavily-lidded eyes were shrewd under their plucked eyebrows and I was suddenly uneasy under the brightness of her gaze.

'It's natural for a person to get homesick sometimes,' I said defensively.

'Perhaps.' She tapped her stick again. 'I wonder why a young bride should find it necessary to sit under a mulberry tree and dream of her old home while her husband is out for the evening. I do wonder at that.'

'Madame la Comtesse!' I spoke on an impulse. 'I am so unhappy that I don't know how I will ever be able to endure it!'

'My dear Madame O'Hara!' She turned her whitecurled head towards me. 'If you are unhappy then there must be some remedy found. What troubles you so?'

'I don't love my husband,' I burst out.

'But how can you possibly know after so short a time?' the countess said.

'I didn't love him when I married him,' I began, but she was tapping her stick impatiently and her voice was brisk.

81

'Marriage is not based upon what the common people call love, surely? Respectable people wed for more important reasons.'

'For money, I suppose?'

'That and because of shared interests,' she nodded. 'Women need a protector and most of them desire children. In order to bear children it is advisable to have a husband.'

'But if one cannot forget another man?'

'Ah!' She drew a long breath and raised her thin eyebrows again. 'So that is the way of it! A foolish infatuation with an unsuitable young man—I've no doubt he was Irish! We all have such men tucked into some corner of our memory. My dear child, you are married now and when you are wed you have licence to dream. In France these matters are arranged in a more civilised manner. The husband has his *maitresse en titre*, the wife her *amour* and they live in mutual harmony.'

'Chas loves me. I don't have any fortune so he married me for affection's sake.'

'Many wives would give a great deal to be in your position.' She patted my hand but I regretted having confided in her. She would never understand how I felt, nor sympathise with a girl who took the only way out of an intolerable situation and then wasted time on regretting it.

'You must count your blessings,' she said. 'You are very young and extremely pretty though your cheeks are a little too red, and your husband seems, from the little I have seen of him, to be a lively young fellow.'

'Who goes out and leaves me to sit alone under a mulberry tree,' I reminded her.

'But as you do not love him,' she returned, 'then you cannot mind his absence!'

She was right of course, and I was being completely illogical but her words didn't make me feel any better. The awful part of it all was that somewhere in the back of my mind was the feeling that if only I had waited for Sabre to come back and confided in him about the coming child he would have married me.

'My own husband was a much older man, but we lived most happily together,' the countess was saying. 'Our château was on the Loire and was most beautiful. There was a lake in the grounds with two black swans sailing upon it. Such a lovely sight they were! When the Terror came my husband insisted that I come to England, and assured me that he would follow later when he settled our affairs. I heard that he had been executed and our château sacked by the mob, but I never learned what happened to the swans. I suspect they were eaten.'

'I'm very sorry,' I said awkwardly.

'So don't talk to me of being unhappy,' she said fiercely. 'When you are old then you may discover that you are also unloved and that is the worst of all!'

I sat for a little while longer while the

garden grew darker and the wind rustled through the branches of the tree. The countess rose, bade me a stately goodnight, and tapped her way up the path, and I too rose, winding my shawl about my head, and went back to the silent, high-ceilinged chambers that were now my home.

Chas came home late that night and I could tell from the way he stumbled over the rug that he'd drunk too much. I had gone to bed and I kept my eyes tightly closed, hoping he would believe me already asleep. I might have known better. Chas had drunk enough to make him belligerent but not enough to make him fall asleep quickly.

He fumbled beneath the covers, and when I smelled the reek on his breath and felt his hand on my bare flesh I turned away sharply, forgetting to feign slumber.

'Fausty, I'm home!' He pulled me into his arms, trying to kiss my ear, but I squirmed away.

'Fausty?' He put his hand under my chin, forcing my head round. 'Fausty, give me a kiss, there's a darling!'

'You're in your cups!' I said, and flung his arm away.

'Can you blame me?' He held me tightly, forcing me back on to the pillow. His face was red and his lank hair flopped over his brow. His hands dug into my shoulders and I was nervous when I felt their strength.

'I'm very tired, Chas.' I spoke as calmly as I could though my heart had begun to race uncomfortably fast. 'I'm truly very weary and don't like—'

'You don't like being mauled. You told me that before! I don't know what ails you— before God I don't! I love you, Fausty. I could have married a rich girl if I'd taken a little trouble!'

'Am I to blame because I have no fortune?' I demanded.

'Of course not, but I did think—you did lead me to believe that you cared for me. Since we married I do begin to wonder if you cared anything at all for me. You never want me to touch you, even when I am sober! Well, tonight is going to be different!'

'It's best that we don't,' I broke in desperately. 'Chas, I'm sorry I've been so horrid! The truth is—I think I'm with child.'

'So soon?' He let me go and stared down into my face. 'Are you certain?'

'Almost certain,' I said. 'It really won't be safe to—to do anything now that might hurt the babe.'

'No, of course not.' He let me go at that and even made a gallant attempt to hide his disappointment. 'But isn't it too early to tell?'

'I am fairly certain,' I said. 'I was sick this morning and my curse is ten days late. I was never late before.'

'A child! By God, but this will please my

father,' he exclaimed. 'He'll very probably increase my allowance. We'll have to hire a serving maid to help you with the work!'

He was so pleased that I felt another stab of guilt but I crushed it down, telling myself that I'd no choice and that in time I'd learn to be a good wife. In time, if only Sabre didn't come back and upset all my resolutions.

CHAPTER FIVE

'Such a lovely surprise to have you call!' Mrs Whitney exclaimed.

'I thought it would be pleasant to visit for an hour.' I drew off my gloves and sat down on the chair she indicated.

'You look very well,' she observed, leaning forward. 'Marriage agrees with you, my dear.'

I was three months pregnant and, though I had not begun to show, my skin glowed and my hair was glossy. Nobody, looking at me, could have guessed that I was anything other than a happy young wife. The truth was that I was bored and miserable and the only thing that gave me any pleasure was the fact that I no longer had to endure Chas's love-making. To avoid that I believe I would have stayed pregnant for ever.

'It's good to see you again,' I smiled at her with real affection.

'I miss you too, dear. My new Sambo is very slow to settle in.' She sighed deeply as if she had been struggling personally with the cares of the household. 'Tell me about your apartments. Are they comfortable?'

'You must come and visit us,' I said.

'Oh, I fear it would be much too exhausting for me,' she said sadly. 'It is in a most desirable neighbourhood, is it not? Have you made any new acquaintances?'

'A French countess lives on the floor above,' I told her.

'A countess!' Mrs Whitney looked suitably impressed. 'You have risen considerably in society since you came to London! My old friend, Georgina, will be delighted to hear of your success, and I do flatter myself that my own efforts to launch you were not entirely in vain.'

She spoke as if I had been her protégé instead of her paid companion, but I didn't begrudge her the little illusion. Illusions matter.

'I shall always be grateful for your kindness,' I said, accepting a glass of negus from Sambo.

'I was only too happy to launch a young lady into the happy estate of matrimony,' she said. 'Charles O'Hara is a very pleasant young gentleman, is he not? Marriage will settle him.'

She nodded her head and looked at me expectantly. I began to tell her about the apartment and some of the things that the

87

countess had told me about her life in Paris before the Revolution. I didn't mention the coming child, deciding to save that for a later occasion, and I made no reference to the difficulties between Chas and me. He spent most of his time out with his various friends and, though he had expressed pleasure at my condition, I knew that he was hurt by my indifference.

A more perceptive woman than Arabel Whitney would have noticed that I spoke a little too fast and a little too cheerfully, but she was not a perceptive person. I rattled on gaily, nineteen to the dozen, while we sipped negus and ate the delicate sugary biscuits of which she was very fond, and she leaned back against the cushions and listened with an occasional comment when she could exert herself sufficiently to make one. The afternoon passed slowly and lazily, with nothing to tempt me back to the apartment. Chas had ridden over to Chelsea Village to see some friends and was not likely to be home for supper.

We were in the midst of our conversation when there was a tap at the door and Sambo announced, 'Mr Sabre to see you, ma'am.'

I had no time in which to prepare myself, or to make an excuse to leave. Sabre walked in, lean and elegant as I remembered him, russet hair waving smoothly against his well-shaped head, grey eyes revealing just the right amount of pleasure at seeing an old friend again.

'Mrs Whitney, you didn't tell me that you were expecting Fausty!' he exclaimed, bowing over her hand and then turning to take mine.

'She came by chance,' Mrs Whitney said, 'and you must call her Mrs O'Hara now. You know that she and Chas were married two months ago?'

'I heard something of it.' He pressed my hand slightly, then took the seat to which she waved him. 'These past three months I've been delayed in the north and now must catch up on the gossip.'

'We missed you at the tables, my dear Sabre,' Mrs Whitney said. 'Was it a romance that kept you so long in Yorkshire?'

'My father has been ill. A slight stroke from which he fortunately recovered, but I had to spend some time running his affairs.'

'He will make a businessman out of you yet,' she said playfully.

'Not if I can avoid it! I am in London for only a few days and then I am expected at a shooting party. The season is already well under way.'

'How fortunate to be unattached and so free to accept all manner of exciting invitations!' Mrs Whitney said. 'But you have not yet congratulated Fausty.'

'It is Chas who is to be congratulated,' he said. 'To Fausty I wish joy.'

'Thank you.' I had collected myself sufficiently to answer him calmly, but my fingers were clenched too tightly around my empty glass.

'I had intended to call upon you,' Sabre said. 'I take it you have moved into Chas's old apartment in Lincoln's Inn Fields.'

'We're settled very comfortably,' I said stiffly.

'Have you met his family? They're very pleasant people.'

'Only his brother, Frank. He was groomsman at the ceremony.'

It was incredible that we should be sitting here at several yards' distance, talking polite banalities.

'And I gave her away,' Mrs Whitney said in a triumphant tone. 'Her own people were not able to come from Ireland.'

'But they're well, I hope?'

'Very well and naturally pleased to hear of my marriage.' I put down the empty glass and rose, drawing on my gloves. 'I ought to be going. Will you have Sambo call a cab for me?'

'Didn't you ride here?' Sabre asked.

'I haven't ridden since my marriage,' I said. 'I hired a gig to bring me here but I sent it away.'

'Then I can kill two birds with one stone,' Sabre informed me, also rising. 'My own coach is at the door so I can escort you home and give Chas my congratulations at the same time.'

'I wouldn't want to inconvenience you,' I

began, but he broke in, his tone firm and pleasant.

'It is never an inconvenience to escort a lovely lady. Mrs Whitney, you and I will have a long talk later on.'

'Are you coming tonight?' she enquired, giving him her hand.

'I may look in later.' He kissed her hand and turned, standing aside to allow me to pass through the door as Sambo held it open.

'Do come and see me again very soon,' Mrs Whitney invited.

I smiled and went out into the passage. I ought to have made some excuse to avoid being alone with him but the truth was that I wanted to be with him and I told myself that it would do no harm. I was going for a short drive with a man who was a friend of my husband's. There was no harm in that!

'So you took my advice,' Sabre said in my ear as he helped me into the coach.

'I married Charles O'Hara.' His hand burned through my sleeve, scorching to the flesh beneath, and despite all my resolutions my voice shook.

'Are you happy?' he asked.

'Much you would care if I were not!' I said.

'So you are not.' He turned his head and gave me a long, thoughtful look. 'I'm sorry, Fausty. I really did hope that you would find contentment.'

'With a man I don't love?'

91

'Chas is a good enough fellow and his family are pleased to see him settled.'

'And your conscience is soothed,' I said, 'so let it rest!'

'You look prosperous,' he said. 'Prosperous and pretty.'

'You don't have to pay me compliments,' I said, moving further from him along the seat.

'Forgive me.' He spoke with a gently deprecating air, but his eyes rested on me with a different expression.

I sat, not returning his look, gazing out of the window at the hot August streets. Without turning my head I was aware of his penetrating regard, and I could feel the colour rising to suffuse my neck and face. It had been a mistake to imagine that he had no further power to stir me.

When we reached our destination I scrambled down before he could offer any help, but he was close behind me as I went up the stairs and unlocked the door that led to our apartments. Sabre had been there before when Chas was a bachelor and he looked round as if he expected to find something changed.

'Will you take a glass of wine?' I asked, aware that his gaze had returned to me.

'Not at the moment, thank you.' He was still staring at me and my eyes met his with unwilling desire.

'Oh, Sabre, why did you push me off on

Chas?' I said miserably. 'Why did you go north and leave me all alone?'

'Hardly alone.' He smiled slightly, tilting my chin towards him. 'I didn't drag you screaming up the aisle to be married to Chas, you know.'

I stared at him, remembering that he didn't know I was pregnant. There was a temptation to tell him warring in me with the guilty feeling that it would do no good at all for poor Chas to learn that he was fathering another man's child. I let the moment slip away and then it was too late for anything because our lips met in a long, passionate embrace. My arms were about his neck and the long length of him pressed against me.

'Where's Chas?' Sabre was tugging off my small hat, winding my dark hair about his fingers.

'He went to see some friends,' I heard myself whisper. 'He won't be back until much later.'

'I missed you, Fausty. All the time I was in Yorkshire, waiting for my father to recover, dealing with family business, I kept the memory of your laughter in my head. I've even woken up at night and reached out in the hope that you were there, but you never were.'

'I am now, Sabre. I'm here now.' I stopped because there were no more words to explain or to excuse, because my garments were crumpled on the floor about my feet. His own clothes joined them and then, the afternoon sunlight gilding us, we walked into the bedroom and all the fumbling caresses I had endured were forgotten.

'I ought not to have let you marry Chas,' Sabre said, when we lay at last side by side, in the quietness of satisfaction.

'You couldn't have prevented it,' I said lazily.

'I could have asked you to be my mistress.' Something inside me cried out, 'Sabre, you could have asked me to be your wife,' but he went on talking, unconscious of hurting me.

'I could have set you up in a little house, settled an annuity on you, visited you often! Instead I let you slip through my fingers as if you were of little account! I might have known that I couldn't get you out of my head!'

I wished I were lodged in his heart but I had enough sense to know that he did not yet love me. He desired me, and desired me the more because I was married to his friend, but he would never marry me while he was still dependent on his father's approval. And I could never hope to marry him because I was already wed of Chas O'Hara.

'I love you, Sabre. You know that I loved you from the beginning,' he said.

'You make it sound like a reproach.' He rolled over to his side and put out his hand to draw me close to him again, but I slipped my legs over the side of the bed and sat up.

'We ought to get dressed. Chas may come

home early. He sometimes does.'

'Only sometimes?' Sabre leaned up on his elbow, his eyes quizzical. 'If I had a wife like you at home I'd come back early.'

'Chas is restless,' I said vaguely.

'You would make any man restless,' he said. 'Come back to bed.'

'There isn't any time.' Fear of discovery, improbable though discovery was, made me curt. I went back into the other room and picked up our garments, wishing that we could remain free and naked for ever. But then I reminded myself that Sabre still considered himself to be free and in taking me he had given nothing of himself.

'If Chas is really neglecting you,' Sabre remarked, reaching for his trousers, 'then he's a fool. With his small fortune he cannot have hoped to catch a great heiress!'

'Oh, we rub along together well enough,' I said, as casually as I could. I didn't want him to look at me with pity.

'But you don't love him.' He pulled his shirt over his head and looked up at me. There was an expression on his face that I was not experienced enough to fathom. I think now that he was torn between pleasure at knowing that I loved him and a complete disregard for the havoc he was causing in my life.

I turned to the mirror to comb my disordered hair and saw my reflection as I had not seen it since I had come to this apartment to live. My eyes were darkly shining, my mouth stung with kisses, my colour high. Even the room looked different. It was hard to imagine being unhappy here.

'Fausty, you know that I'm going back up north in a few days?' Sabre questioned.

'To a shooting party, yes.'

'I don't want to lose you,' he said.

'You don't want to lose me!' I swung about, taking refuge in indignation. 'Mother of God, Earl Sabre, but you were the one who gave me up! You were the one who said your family would cut you off without a penny if you wed a poor Irish girl! You were the one who told me to marry Chas O'Hara! And now you come back and tell me that you don't want to lose me?'

'I'll come back,' he began, but I shook my head violently.

'I don't want you to come back, Sabre! I never want to see you again. It's wrong and selfish of you to come back and take what you passed on to your friend!'

'We are both selfish,' he said lightly. 'I'm a selfish fellow, my dear love, and you are an Irish maiden determined to rise in the world! We are two of a kind.'

I was silent, knowing there was some truth in what he said. He had used me, but I had allowed myself to be used, and unless I made an end of it he would come back to me again and again until there was nothing left for the man I had married.

'I want you to stay away from me,' I said walking rapidly to the bed and beginning to straighten the covers. 'I want you to leave me in peace, Sabre. You had the chance to marry me and I wasn't good enough for you. Well, it's too late now! You gave me to Chas and you can't steal me back when the fancy takes you!'

'If you were happy with him you'd never have let me touch you.'

'And if you had any affection for me or your friend you'd not have tempted me to betray him!'

We stood on opposite sides of the bed on which we had just made love and glared at each other, trapped in the need to hurt so that we could forget our own guilt, and in that tense moment the outer door opened and Chas called.

'Fausty, I'm home!'

I couldn't have felt worse if Sabre and I had still been mother naked between the rumpled sheets. As it was, I stood frozen, staring at Sabre, and then my voice came back in a rush and I hurried out.

'Chas! Come and see who's come to visit!'

'I owe you a wedding present,' Sabre said, strolling out to grip Chas by the hand.

'I was showing Sabre round the apartment,' I said. 'We met by chance when I visited Mrs Whitney.'

I had spoken too fast and too loud. Chas

shot me a faintly puzzled look and said, 'Sabre's been here before. There's no need to give him a conducted tour.'

'I was hoping there'd be a glass of some reviving liquid at the end of it,' Sabre drawled.

'For the Lord's sake, Fausty, haven't you given the man a drink yet?' Chas went to the sideboard and rooted for a bottle and glasses. 'You'll stay for supper, Sabre? Fausty's not much of a cook, but we've progressed past Irish stew in the last few weeks.'

'I'm engaged elsewhere this evening,' Sabre said, taking the proffered drink and sitting down in the deep armchair where Chas usually lounged. 'I ran into your pretty bride over at Arabel's and had the pleasure of bringing her home. I was hoping to catch you before I set off again.'

'Back to Yorkshire? You've only just come back to London!'

'I'm promised to friends for a week or two, and then I have to look in on the family again. My father's been ill.'

'I heard something of it,' Chas nodded. 'Not serious, I hope?'

'A stroke. Oh, he's nearly over it, but he's past sixty and I am the only son so he frets about the future. I've tried to take an interest in the mill, to please him, but it bores me stupid to be up to my ears in wool prices!'

'You should take a wife,' Chas said airily. 'I can recommend it. We can both recommend it, can't we, Fausty?'

I could say nothing. Instead I smiled weakly and fiddled with my hair.

'You both look well on it,' Sabre said easily.

'And in the spring—' Chas began, but I interrupted him gaily.

'Don't waste the rest of the day going on about the joys of wedded bliss when you know you don't mean half of it! Why did you come home so early? Was Chelsea not amusing?'

'Amusing but unprofitable,' Chas said.

'You haven't lost again!' I exclaimed.

'Not much, so you needn't begin to nag,' he said. 'If I'd stayed on I could have won it all back and more, but I decided to come home, so I'd appreciate a welcome. You'd not believe this, Sabre, but I don't always get an open-armed greeting from my ever-loving wife!'

'Why don't I take both of you over to the Vauxhall Gardens for a bite of supper?' Sabre drawled.

There was amusement in his grey eyes. It would flatter his conceit, I knew, to watch us squabbling. He was a dog in the manger as far as I was concerned, not wanting me entirely for himself but not wanting me to be truly happy with Chas either. I was determined not to give him that satisfaction.

'You and Chas go,' I said. 'I've a lot of sewing to catch up on. Anyway you'll likely end up playing dice at Mrs Whitney's and that's not my notion of a lively evening.'

'Are you sure you don't mind?' Chas said uncertainly.

'You'll have lots to talk about anyway,' I said brightly. 'Sabre's leaving for the north again and it will be months before you have the chance of meeting up!'

'If you're sure you don't mind,' Chas said.

'I'll get a clean shirt for you,' I said and whisked into the bedroom.

I was rummaging in the drawer when Chas came in, closing the door behind him, and beginning to strip off his shirt.

'You're in a queer mood,' he said, glancing at me. 'Why did you stop me telling Sabre about the babe?'

'I want to keep it a secret,' I said.

'For heaven's sake, why?' He caught the shirt I tossed him. 'It's natural enough for a married couple to have a baby!'

'I don't want everybody gossiping,' I objected. 'I know what men are like, worse than old women when it comes to sniggering and making faces behind other folks' back! It's too soon anyway. There's something—not very nice about getting pregnant so soon after the ceremony. I'm not sure it's respectable.'

'As respectable as inviting a man into your bedchamber,' Chas began.

'Meaning what exactly!' I swung round, shutting the drawer with a sharp click.

'Meaning nothing,' Chas said, looking surprised. 'It was just a casual remark, that's all. What on earth is the matter with you? Anyone would think that you didn't like Sabre! Why, if it hadn't been for him you and I might never have met and married!'

'And I'm supposed to thank him for that?'

'It's your condition,' Chas said. 'It makes women nervous and unsure of themselves. Frank tells me that Sybil is exactly the same when she's expecting.'

'Damn Sybil,' I muttered.

'Look, if you don't want anybody to know,' Chas said, heavily patient, 'I'll not breathe a word of it, even to Sabre. Are you sure that you don't mind being left here this evening?'

'I shall be very glad of a little peace,' I said.

'I'll go down and bring some wood for the fire,' Chas said.

'Oh, don't be such a fool, Chas! It's the height of summer and the fire's not even lit!' I said in exasperation.

I was trying to please you,' he said, 'but nothing I do pleases you, does it? You are determined to remain in a thoroughly bad humour, so I may as well go out and enjoy myself with an old friend.'

'And you'll not be gossiping about my condition?' I persisted.

'Not one word. There! does that please you?' he demanded.

'Yes, I'm sorry, Chas. I'm in a foul mood today,' I said in belated apology. 'I think I got tired going to Mrs Whitney's.'

'You ought to take better care of yourself, dear.' He gave me a perfunctory kiss on the cheek and opened the door again, speaking cheerfully as he went into the other room. 'Forgive me for the delay, Sabre! I can never find a clean shirt when I need one.'

'Chas, will you go down and send my coach away?' Sabre enquired. 'It's a pleasant evening and I've a fancy to ride if there's a horse to be hired.'

'I'll get you one from the livery stable at the end of the street,' Chas said promptly. 'Keep Fausty company for a few minutes.'

He went out, happy to please his friend, and Sabre looked across at me with a raised eyebrow.

'Won't you change your mind and come with us?' he enquired. 'I promise you a good supper.'

'I'll eat a better one alone!' I said sharply.

'Darling, what ails you?' He put down his glass, and came to me, putting his hand under my chin and tilting my face. 'Not an hour ago you and I were sweet as doves, and now you snap and snarl like an evil-tempered shrew! What's wrong?'

'I said I didn't want to see you again,' I said.

'But you do love me?'

'You know that!' I jerked my head away from his hand, the words tumbling out of me. 'You could have married me, Sabre, but you chose to go away instead. You told me to marry Chas and I married him! Now you come back and expect to start again from where we left off, but it's over! I ought never to have let you bring me home. That was wrong but it won't happen again. I won't let it happen, because it's not fair to Chas or to me. It's not fair, Sabre!'

'So!' He let his hands drop and sent me a look of mingled exasperation and amusement. 'The Irish wind blows cold today, does it?'

'And will continue freezing,' I said coldly.

'So!' He repeated the exclamation softly and then laughed.

'Let us see how long you keep your resolve to be a true and faithful wife to poor old Chas!'

'He married me.'

'And deserves your gratitude. Of course he does! But I don't think you will dislodge me so easily from your mind, my dear Fausty.'

'I shall try,' I said tensely, moving to the outer door and opening it.

'Good-evening to you, Mrs O'Hara.' He swept a bow that was more insulting than polite and went past me down the stairs.

CHAPTER SIX

The wisest course for me to follow was to put Earl Sabre right out of my mind and fill my head with wifely devotion and thoughts of the coming child. It was simple to make such a resolve but impossible to carry out. In the weeks and months that followed I tried very hard to be a good wife, and naturally I failed. It wasn't all my fault. Chas, having pleased his parents by taking a wife, proceeded to carry on as if he were still a bachelor. Oh, he gave me money to buy food and clothes and things for the baby, and a foolish excuse on his lips. There were days when I was left alone for hours while he was off with his friends, racing his curricle or his horse, rowing on the Thames or getting his nose bloodied in the boxing ring. If I had made the apartment more welcoming perhaps he would have come home earlier and stayed longer, but in a way I was glad of his frequent absences because it was better to be alone than to have to keep up some kind of conversation with him.

I bought a lot of clothes for the coming child because I wanted to make the baby more real to myself. I was determined to love it as passionately as I had loved Sabre. It was safe to love a small child, but men like Earl Sabre, who took what they fancied when they felt like it, were dangerous to love, dangerous even to think about. And so I sat and thought about him, remembering how his dark red hair lay in deep, crisp waves over his head and how his eyes gleamed silver-grey between their russet lashes.

There were letters, two from Mrs Flannigan who wrote to tell me that Mary had been accepted into the novitiate, and wrote again to congratulate me on my coming child. I read these two letters over and over, picturing them all at home and wondering why I had ever been fool enough to leave.

The countess, whose old eyes were sharp, had speedily divined both my pregnancy and my unhappiness, and fallen into the habit of coming down to sit with me when Chas was out. She was a tiresome old woman in many ways, forever telling me about the grandeur of her former life and of how, if only she had had the foresight to smuggle out her jewels, she would not now be forced to exist in a shabby apartment. But she had a kindly side to her nature though it was usually hidden under an exceedingly sharp tongue.

We were sitting together one afternoon. The first snow had fallen and Chas had taken it into his head to go skating. I was far too big and clumsy to go walking for very long, and skating was out of the question. Instead I sat, knitting in hand, a shawl only partly concealing my bulge, and the countess glanced across at me, her white curled head on one side, and said.

'Who is going to deliver the child? With a first one it is advisable to engage a physician.'

'I hadn't thought about it,' I said blankly. 'At home the older women generally help at the birthing.'

'You are not among barbarians now,' the old lady said crisply, 'but in a civilised city! A young lady of breeding should have the attentions of a qualified physician. When is the child due?'

'February, March,' I said. 'I'm not absolutely certain. First babies are often early, you know.'

'Never had one, so I'll take your word for it.' She cast me another sharp glance and said, 'You look very big for someone with four months still to go.'

'I have big hips,' I said defensively.

'You're not eating properly. You should be eating for two, you know.'

'I'm eating very well,' I said impatiently. 'You fuss too much, Madame.'

'Someone has to fuss,' she said serenely. 'That husband of yours takes little enough interest in you. Oh, it will probably be different when the baby comes, especially if it's a boy. A man does like to have a son.'

'I don't care what it is.' I threw aside the knitting and rose, pulling my shawl more tightly round my shoulders. 'All I want is to get it over and done.'

'And then you will be living happily after ever?'

'Why not?' I turned to face her.

'Child, it doesn't work like that,' she said. 'I remember once you told me there was a man you couldn't forget—'

'I've forgotten him!'

'Of course you have,' she nodded. 'That's why you are so brimful of happiness now. Child, when will you learn that you cannot forget simply for the wishing? You are not happy with your husband. Why pretend that you are? It's better to admit that you're miserable and then start again from there.'

'With what?' I asked.

'With the child, if you like. Your husband may settle down when the child is born and even take up a profession. I would not normally advise any gentleman to go into a paid occupation but Mr O'Hara would benefit, I believe, by having something to do. You have not yet visited his family?'

I shook my head.

'After the child comes the two of you ought to go into the country for a little while,' she said. 'Country air is very good for the young, and there are fewer opportunities for gambling there. This man you have forgotten—do you ever see him?'

'Not for many months. He went north again.'

'Then I hope he stays there,' she said firmly.

'I have forgotten him,' I repeated. 'I don't expect ever to see him again and I'm very pleased that he can't see me at the moment. I never felt so ugly in my life!'

'Your cheeks are still distressingly red,' the

countess said, 'but you are very far from ugly, my dear.'

'Thank you.' On impulse I stood to kiss her cheek, but she drew herself upright, saying heartily,

'My dear, in the court of King Louis only those related within the fourth degree of consanguinity are permitted to embrace on the cheek. However, in Ireland such delicate shades of behaviour are probably not observed. Now, you must find a good, reliable physician and make certain he attends you during your confinement. I myself will make some enquiries on your behalf.'

'That's very kind of you,' I said.

'And I've a little gift for the child,' she said, drawing a small packet from the depths of the reticule at her skirt.

I sat down again and opened it, my eyes widening as I saw the gold bracelet on its bed of velvet.

'It was one of the few pieces I was able to bring out of France,' she said.

'But it's very valuable, Madame!' I exclaimed. 'I couldn't possibly accept it.'

'Put it away safely.' She patted my arm briskly. 'If you have a daughter the bracelet will suit her beautifully when she is old enough to go to balls, and if you have a son, he will take a bride one day!'

'Thank you, Madame.' I looked again at the intricately chased circle of gold.

'Put it away, put it away!' She reached for her stick and rose, waving me back into my seat when I would have risen with her. 'Rest your feet as often as possible and don't show that to your husband. A lady should always keep a little in reserve, against emergencies.'

When she had gone I hid the gold bracelet under the nightgowns and caps I'd made for the baby. It was kicking vigorously under my heart and for the first time I thought of it as a person who would one day live separate from me in the world. Whatever my own unhappiness the child deserved a peaceful home with two parents who showed affection to each other.

When Chas came home I had supper ready for him and I'd put a blue ribbon in my hair, but one look at his face told me the evening's gaming had gone badly.

'How much did you lose?' I began, but he was pulling off coat and cravat and answered me irritably.

'Don't start the moment I step through the door, Fausty! I've had a run of bad luck. I know it already and I don't need you to tell me about it all over again!'

'Your supper's ready.'

'Meaning that I'm late? No need to tell me that either. Anyway, I had a bite at Mrs Whitney's. She sends her regards and says if the weather wasn't so cold she would pay you a visit.'

'Would you like something to drink?' I asked.

'I've had sufficient already.' He sat down and began to tug off his boots. 'Why are you being so attentive? Most evenings you are either asleep or tight-lipped over a piece of knitting when I get home.'

'I've resolved to be more loving in future.' I came to the side of the chair and knelt by him, my tone as gentle as I could make it. 'Chas, I've been thinking and it seems to me that I could have been a better wife. We ought to get along well together since we are married and there's a child coming.'

'It isn't my fault if we can't get on well together,' Chas said. 'I wed you because I fell in love with you, Fausty, and you've never shown me much affection, not even when we first wed!'

'And I might have shown more affection if you were not always elsewhere, tossing dice or sorting wagers!' I said, stung by his tone.

'You would like me to find a position of some kind, I suppose? It would satisfy you to have me chained down to some futile employment from dawn to dusk.'

'Other men work!'

'Not gentlemen,' he said. 'I sometimes wonder if you ever met any gentlemen before you came to England.'

'My dadda is as fine a gentlemen as any jumped-up English dandy,' I said, forgetting to

110

be gentle as I struggled to my feet.

'Are there any Irish gentlemen?' Chas drawled.

'Better ones than I've ever met in England!' I flared. 'And that includes you, Charles O'Hara! You and all your friends who waste time instead of spending it!'

'Oh, I know you don't like my friends!' Chas flung his boots across the room and glared at me sullenly. 'Even Sabre was frozen out when he came!'

'Have you news of him?' I couldn't help asking eagerly.

'Of Sabre? Not a word since he went north. Why do you ask?'

'You mentioned him.'

'As an example. Why should you be interested in Sabre's doings?'

'I'm not,' I said, too quickly, because he was looking at me with a puzzled frown that might turn at any moment to suspicion.

'Well, I've heard nothing,' Chas said. 'Sabre was never much of a one for writing letters. I do have other friends, you know. Gentlemen, Fausty, whom I'd bring home to visit if there was a welcome waiting.'

'I don't wish to meet anyone, not looking like this,' I said crossly.

'You never wanted to meet them before your shape changed!' he retorted. 'I swear I never knew a married lady so missish before! Perhaps you're ashamed to be carrying my

111

child?'

'Don't be foolish,' I began, but he interrupted me, his voice rising, his broad face reddening.

'Foolish! Before God, but I begin to think I was foolish to take you as a wife at all! I don't even know how I managed to get you with child for you've never welcomed me in your bed. I wonder why you accepted me in the first place. There are not many men who would take a bride from a bog.'

'A bog! I was never in a bog in my life!'

'Who only knows how to cook Irish stew!'

'Tonight I cooked mutton chops,' I said.

'Which probably taste the same,' Chas said.

'Then don't eat them!' I cried.

We stood, glowering at each other, and then with a muffled oath Chas seized the dish of chops and threw them against the wall.

If he had hoped to intimidate me by a show of temper then he'd chosen the wrong person for I was never one to be bullied. Before the fragments had all scattered over the floor I'd lifted the steaming dish of carrots and flung them in the same direction.

There were footsteps running up the outside stairs and someone pounding on the door. Chas, darting me a furious look, strode across the room and opened the door. It was Mr Pettifer, the young lawyer, who stood there, peering anxiously in.

'Is anything wrong?' he enquired, his eyes

moving past Chas to where the shattered dishes and the remains of the meal lay.

'My wife has had a slight accident,' Chas said.

'Oh.' Mr Pettifer's eyes continued to move from the broken dishes to where I stood, breathing hard, my fists clenched. Then he said 'Oh' again.

'Nerves, old fellow,' Chas said, lowering his voice slightly but still remaining audible to me. 'Ladies will have them at certain times. You know how it is!'

'Yes, of course.' Mr Pettifer looked highly embarrassed. 'I had no intention of intruding, sir, but my wife and I heard the er—noise and feared some mishap.'

'None in the world!' Chas said, clapping the other on the shoulder. 'We must allow the ladies their little foibles.'

He did not, of course, volunteer the information that he had instigated the row. I marched into the bedroom and relieved my feelings by slamming the door behind me. Outside a fresh flurry of snow beat against the window-panes. The fire had burned low while I waited for Chas to come home and there were specks of black soot all over the hearth. I poked the coals savagely, watching a shower of red sparks fly up the chimney, thinking of gentler peat fires and of the warmth and bustle I had left in order to come and live with a man whom I not only didn't love but was beginning actively to dislike.

The winter dragged on. The snow, delicate as lace when it fell, quickly became a morass of trodden slush and soon the sharp, piercing rain of January washed away the little Christmas cheer there had been in our apartment. I was too big to move about with ease anywhere and, to add to my misery, my ankles swelled and my legs ached. My great dread was that Sabre might come back to London for I had a horror of his seeing me in this condition, but he didn't come and there was no word of him.

I had expected none and it was better so, but the days were so long and lonely and only in my dreams was I slim and pretty again. Chas had fallen out of love with me completely. I think now he had never really been in love with me at all. He had liked the idea of being in love with a pretty young woman who, being poor, would not expect too much attention once the ceremony was over. He had married, I thought bitterly, because his family wanted him to settle down and I was probably the only one who would take him.

'I'm going out for an hour,' he broke into my thoughts to say.

'What? Oh, very well.' I answered him vaguely, not troubling to turn my head.

'I thought I might look in at White's,' he said.

'You could look in at the fishmonger's too,' I said. 'We've not much for supper.'

114

'I can get a bite at White's,' Chas said.

'While I starve I suppose.' I did turn my head then to scowl at him.

There was always an instant just before I set eyes on Chas—a moment when I hoped by some miracle he might have changed, and always there was the same sickening let down when I saw the same broad freckled face and lank fair hair set on the wide shoulders with the disproportionately thin legs.

'Surely you've some food in?' he said.

'Some cold meat and fruit but we need bread.'

'Other wives manage to do their own marketing,' he grumbled.

'Other wives have maids,' I reminded him. 'We have never been able to afford a servant.'

'At home in Ireland you had butlers and a footman, I suppose?'

'I expected better when I married! Chas, surely you can come home early and get some fish on the way!' I pleaded, weary of the constant bickering.

'Why don't you go upstairs and have supper with the countess?' he suggested. 'The poor old dear is always pleased to see you.'

'The countess hasn't been well.'

'All the more reason for you to go up and sit with her. I will try not to be late.' He flung his greatcoat about his shoulders, pecked my cheek, and went out. Any hope I might have had of his bringing back some fish vanished with the slamming of the door.

After a while I got up, pulled my thick shawl about me, for the staircase was chilly, and went up to the apartment where the countess lived in a shabby gentility. Her door was on the latch and the first thing I heard as I pushed it wider was the sound of her coughing.

'Madame, are you sick?' I went to her as quickly as I could, but she shook her head, looking up at me with fever-bright eyes from the chair in which she was huddled.

'A slight rheum, nothing to signify,' she wheezed.

'The fire needs building up,' I said, looking at the hearth disparagingly. 'Where's the lad?'

She paid an urchin down the street to bring up firewood once or twice a week but the log-basket held only a few chips.

'Foolish lad broke his ankle and cannot get about.' She coughed again, scarlet-faced.

'I'll go down and see if the timber-cart's on the road.' I bent to tug the big basket from its place by the hearth. 'If it's not there shall I bring some coal?'

'Not coal! I cannot afford coal fires,' she said fretfully.

'Wood then! I'll bring some and build up the fire. We could have some hot soup.'

'*Ma petite,* you must not tire yourself out in running after an old woman,' she said, but there was no real force in her voice.

I pulled the log-basket through the door. It

116

was not heavy but it was unwieldy and I must have bent down too quickly because I had an unpleasant, niggling pain in the small of my back. I humped the basket in front of the bulge where my trim waist had been and made my way down the stairs but when I reached my own landing the pain came again so sharply that I had to put the basket down and lean against the wall, biting my lip to avoid crying out.

There were some logs in our coal-scuttle mixed with the coal and the twists of paper I used to kindle the fires. I would take some of those up, I decided, and not risk a trip down into the freezing street. I was loading the cut logs into the basket when the stabbing agony caught me a third time and I retched miserably as it twisted through me. Dear God, but it couldn't be the babe. Babies took hours and hours to be born and mine wasn't due for another month. I hadn't even done anything about engaging a physician.

I pulled myself upright and went out on to the landing, leaning over to call as loudly as I could for Mrs Pettifer, uttering a silent prayer of thanks when the door opened and she came out, raising her face to mine.

'Mrs O'Hara, is anything wrong?' she called anxiously.

'Madame La Comtesse is not well. She needs her fire building up and some hot soup making. I am not able to do it myself.' I broke off as the pain gripped me again.

'Is the child coming? John!' She turned her head to shout his name.

'I don't need a lawyer,' I said, finding a gleam of humour in the situation. 'I am more in need of a physician.'

'John is always very calm in moments of crisis. *John!*' She called him again and came rustling up the stairs towards me. 'You had best lie down and I will boil some water! I am not experienced in the birthing of babies but one always requires boiling water. *John!*'

'What is it, my love?' The lawyer must have been deep in his studies or dozing for he came out blinking, his hair and cravat awry.

'The countess is sick and Mrs O'Hara is having her baby,' she called, putting an arm about me and helping me through the door of my own rooms. She was a thin, small young woman and I felt like a large sailing ship being towed along by a very small rowing-boat.

'See to the countess first,' I said through gritted teeth. 'Babies take hours and hours to be born.'

'You lie down, Mrs O'Hara.' Mr Pettifer relieved his wife of her burden. 'Run up to the old lady, my love, and see what can be done for her.'

'There's wood in the basket,' I pointed.

'I'll take it up, John, we must boil some water!' She took up the basket and went out.

'If I can lie down,' I said, trying to think

clearly through a haze of pain, 'I will feel better, I'm sure.'

'Where is your husband?' Mr Pettifer was enquiring. 'At a time like this—'

'At a time like this,' I said, 'my dear husband is out gambling at White's or some other den, and would be completely useless even if you found him. Do you know of a good physician?'

'There is one three streets off. I know him by reputation only. My wife will be down very shortly.'

'And the babe will be here shortly after,' I said, and a spasm held me fast again. 'I feel a very great desire to push.'

'Oh?' He had helped me to the bed and was piling quilts round me.

'Do run for the physician and beg him to come quickly,' I implored. 'I don't think this baby is going to take hours after all.'

'I really think your husband ought to be with you at a time like this,' he said, shifting from one foot to the other.

'Mother of God, but he would be quite useless!' I exclaimed. 'Do hurry, Mr Pettifer! The babe will be here while you're still dithering.'

'My wife will be down almost at once,' he said, and fled.

I tried to twist myself into a more comfortable position, but the quilts were stifling and the pain was so bad that I couldn't stay still for more than a few minutes. I tried desperately to remember what it had been like when my mother had had her babies, but we children had always been shooed out of the cabin and only allowed back when the child had been washed and wrapped up in a swaddling blanket.

The pain was tearing through me and all I wanted to do was to bear down as hard as I could. I was aware of Mrs Pettifer running back into the room and wringing her hands helplessly. I wanted to tell her to send for Earl Sabre so that he could see the damage he had done, but I had sufficient sense to keep silent. What mattered now was that this wretched child should be safely born and that I should recover. I was determined to recover.

'The countess is feeling much better,' Mrs Pettifer said.

'Good for the countess.' I tried to smile but my lips were stiff and my eyes wouldn't focus properly. I heard more footsteps running up the stairs and then the lawyer's breathless voice.

'The physician will be here in a few minutes. We are to boil some water, my dear. Your baby is two months early, is it not, Mrs O'Hara? It will likely be small and need warmth, so you'd best get more coal and wood for the fire. Mrs O'Hara, are you certain you wouldn't like me to fetch your husband? At a time like this—'

I don't want him at any time!' I said through my teeth, and then the pain overcame me and there was no room in me for anything but the labour of bearing Sabre's child. Children. Before midnight I was delivered of a son and a daughter both perfect, both with dark red hair that already lay thick and smooth against their tiny, well-shaped heads.

CHAPTER SEVEN

'I shall give them Irish names,' I said firmly.

'Don't I have any choice in the matter?' Chas, who had been reading a news journal, folded it with irritable crackling noises.

'A man who cannot be bothered to come home to help with the birthing of his child forfeits that choice,' I said.

'Be fair, do! How was I to know you'd go early into labour?'

'And when you did condescend to come home,' I went on unheeding, 'you were in your cups! You were so deep in them that when you saw the babies you were convinced that you were seeing double!'

'I've not been drunk since the babies were born,' he said sullenly.

'Congratulations,' I said. 'They're a week old so the effort must have been enormous!'

'Lord, but you've a bitter tongue, Fausty!' he exclaimed. 'Motherhood is supposed to soften a woman, but it's made you hard as nails! Well, what are they to be called then?'

'Patrick and Gobnait,' I said. 'After my grandparents.'

'Nobody is going to mistake them for anything but Irish with names like that,' he said wryly. 'Patrick O'Hara and Gobnait O'Hara! I'll go round and see the priest about the baptism. I've written to Frank to ask him to be godfather.'

'And the countess to be godmother,' I said.

'Sybil had another boy,' Chas said. 'It was a disappointment, but next time they may be more fortunate.'

'Next time? Poor Sybil!' I said feelingly.

'Oh, I don't suppose bearing a child is as bad as women make out,' he said cheerfully. 'Look at you! Already on your feet! The physician was delighted with your progress!'

'I heard him,' I said. 'He told you that I was a strapping wench who could bear a child every year and not notice it. Well, the next one you will have to bear all by yourself because I don't intend to have any more!'

'Sybil always says that,' Chas remarked.

'I mean it,' I said flatly. 'Two are quite sufficient. I don't know how we are going to manage as it is!'

'My father is bound to increase my allowance,' Chas said airily.

'So that you will have more to waste on dice and horse races,' I muttered.

'Well, if I'm to be denied my rights as a

husband I shall have to occupy my time somehow,' he informed me.

'Do as you please.' I shrugged and turned my attention again to the babies.

I had expected to love my child but I had not expected to feel such an intense devotion that nothing else seemed to matter. The pain and confusion of their delivery was already fading in my mind and I was swiftly regaining my strength.

'The physician said they were the biggest seven-month twins he'd ever seen in his life.' Chas had come to my side and was looking down at the two drawers which we had utilised as cradles.

'We run to big babies in our family,' I said lightly.

'They're lively enough.' He was still gazing down at them and after a moment he said reflectively, 'We don't have any red hair in the family.'

'I'm dark and you're fair, so it's probably a compromise,' I said. 'Their hair will change shade anyway. Babies' hair always does.'

'That shade looks fixed.'

'Much you know about babies!' I scoffed. We were suddenly on dangerous ground and I wasn't sure how to avoid the marsh at my feet.

'Twins are generally smaller. I know that much,' he said.

'So I'm to be blamed for having healthy babies, am I?' I retorted. 'There is no pleasing you at all, Charles O'Hara.'

'I'm sorry, Fausty.' He made a move to take my hand but I stooped instead to pick up one of the babies, and after a moment he turned and went out.

I had hoped that once the birth was over I might be able to settle down in my own mind as Chas's wife, but the truth was that I could hardly endure to have him come near me.

The babies were given the names I had chosen and Frank came over from his own family to stand as godfather to them both. I had liked Frank when we had met at the wedding but now, when I looked at him, I was reminded of poor Sybil who had not yet succeeded in bearing him a daughter, and he seemed smug and less sympathetic than before.

'You must coax my brother to bring you to visit us as soon as the babies are old enough to be taken on a journey,' he said. 'My parents are anxious to see their grandchildren and to meet their new daughter-in-law.'

'Not so new,' I said.

'But already a mother, eh?' He nudged me with his elbow, lowering his voice to add, 'To tell you the truth, I never would have thought that Chas had it in him. Always shy with ladies of his own station, and now seven-month bouncing twins, by God!'

'But—Chas and I never—!' I began indignantly, and stopped, flushing deeply as I caught his knowing glance. There was no doubt that he imagined that Chas and I had had to be wed. ' I do beg you not to tease Chas about it,' I finished lamely.

'Not one word, my dear sister-in-law.' He laid a finger along the side of his nose and in the gesture I read his changed opinion of me. Worse was to follow. Sauntering across to where the Pettifers stood, sipping the champagne we had bought for the christening party, he observed cheerfully,

'I wish it were possible for me to stay longer, and make closer friendship with my brother's neighbours. I believe I have you good people to thank for the safe delivery of my niece and nephew.'

'We were happy to be of help,' Mrs Pettifer said. 'They are most beautiful children.'

'That they are,' he agreed heartily, 'though the Lord knows where they got their hair from! There isn't any red hair in our family. That particular shade is very distinctive, wouldn't you agree?'

He meant no harm by his remarks. For all he knew I had left a crowd of red-headed brothers and sisters back in Ireland. But I saw Chas glance in my direction, the faint suspicion dawning in his face, and I heard my own voice raised too quickly and too brightly.

'We must hope the shade will darken or poor Gobnait will never catch a husband!'

'Such an unusual name,' the countess said.

125

Recovered from her chill she sat like some enthroned queen sporting a feather hat that was slightly too grand to look ridiculous.

'It is the Gaelic for Abigail, Madame,' I told her.

'Quite charming.' She inclined her head slightly. 'I am certain she will grow up to be exceedingly pretty and have many suitors.'

'We might even marry her off to Sabre,' Chas said.

'Oh, no!' I heard myself exclaim, and then my voice babbled on. 'Earl Sabre will be far too old by the time Gobnait's of marriageable age and, in any case, I would hate to have my daughter go so far north. Madam, you must have another glass of champagne! Chas, we are neglecting our guests!'

If I had been older and more experienced I could have hidden my guilt more cleverly, but I was scarcely eighteen and my guilt weighed on me too heavily. I went too swiftly to fill up the glasses and pass round the slices of iced cake that little Mrs Pettifer had baked for the occasion and it seemed to me that the twins' hair glowed redder and Chas watched me with an ever-deepening suspicion.

Frank was starting for home again that same day and I was not sorry to see him leave. I didn't like him as well as I had liked him before and my only regret was that Chas was not going with him. On the other hand there was the possibility that the two of them might, in the course of conversation, draw certain conclusions. I dared not risk that.

'As soon as the weather is warm enough to permit the babies a change of air, you must come and visit us, mind,' he said, kissing my cheek as he took his leave.

I murmured something polite and he threw his arm about Chas's shoulders as they went towards the door. Watching, I noticed him slip a small packet into the other's hand. No doubt it was money from their father and I had equally no doubt at all that I would see none of it.

'A wonderful afternoon.' The countess was rising and tapping her way to the door. I thanked her, and she flicked my cheek with a still elegant forefinger, shrewdness in her eyes as she said, 'And it is good to see you take such comfort in your children.'

So that was to be my lot. A husband whom I could neither respect nor like and all my consolation derived from two small babies. For a young girl it was a cheerless prospect.

'That went off very well,' Chas said, closing the door on the last of the guests. He poured himself another drink.

'Patrick and Gobnait behaved like angels,' I agreed.

'Like their mother?' He gave me a glance. 'You are a good, faithful wife, aren't you, Fausty?'

'Yes, I am.' It was almost true, I thought.

'Fausty, why didn't you want Sabre to know you were pregnant?' he asked abruptly.

' I didn't like Sabre very much.'

'Not like him? You were out riding with him when we first met!'

'Only because I didn't know anyone else in London.'

'And Sabre stayed up north after he visited here. He's never stayed away from London so long before.'

'How should I know why he stayed away?' I said. 'Write to him and ask him if you're so interested! But don't put me through an inquisition about a man I don't even like.'

'Sabre has red hair,' Chas said.

I felt myself stiffen and the palms of my hands were suddenly cold with seat. My voice didn't sound like my own as I said, 'What on earth is that supposed to mean? Are you already in your cups or something?'

'I mention the fact as a deuced odd coincidence, that's all,' he said. 'Don't you think it's a strange coincidence, my dear wife?'

'I think you're not making any sense,' I said, summoning all my control and moving to sit by the fire. 'I do promise you there are thousands of red-haired men in the land.'

'But only one I can think of whom you know,' he said, watching me still over the rim of the glass.

'Are you going to drink for the rest of the day?' I enquired. 'There's still half a bottle of champagne left but it'll likely be flat by now.'

'Fausty, tell me the truth.' He put down the glass and came to me. 'There never was anything between you and Sabre, was there?'

'That's an insulting question and I don't have to answer it,' I said, but my words ended in a gasp as he seized my wrists and pulled me up to face him.

'Does that mean you can't answer it?' he demanded.

'It means that I won't!' I tugged fruitlessly but his hands were strong and I couldn't break free.

'Are the twins truly seven-months babes?' he asked. 'The physician couldn't credit it.'

'I bore the twins,' I said, meeting his gaze with an angrily defiant one of my own. 'I ought to know how early they came! My God, Chas, but you pretend to love me and you go out of your way to say such things to me as any decent husband would shame to even think! You disgust me with your suspicions! Do you think you can cover up your own bad behaviour by accusing me of worse?'

'They don't look like me,' he said sulkily, dropping my hands.

'They don't look like anyone yet!' I said, rubbing my wrists where he had gripped them. 'Chas, you're behaving like a jealous fool, and you've no cause! We have neither of us laid eyes on Sabre since last summer, so how can you possibly imagine I am nourishing some tender—I don't know what you would call it but I call it a very great nonsense!'

'I think I'll step over to White's,' he said.

'Every time you lose an argument,' I said, 'you run off to your friends who fleece you of your money while they tell you what a fine fellow you are! Frank gave you some money as he was leaving, didn't he?'

'My father sent something extra,' Chas admitted.

'That was intended for the babies,' I said sharply. 'It must have been!'

'It was intended for me to use as I see fit.'

'So you'll gamble it? Is it any wonder that I can't look on you with any affection?' I demanded.

I might as well have been talking to myself, for in the middle of the sentence, Chas walked out, slamming the door so hard that one of the twins woke up and started to cry.

The snow had turned to rain, lashing down on the pavements, bouncing up from the cobbles and cornices. There were only dregs and crumbs left of the christening party and, looking at them, I was filled with melancholy. The English didn't really know how to celebrate, I thought, wistfully remembering the excitement of festivals back home. I was sick of London, sick of being the well-bred uncomplaining wife. More than anything I longed to go home for a while. There was no reason why I should not, I thought, reaching for pen and paper. I would write and tell Mrs Flannigan my news so that she could pass it on to the family. My spirits rose slightly as I wrote, the mere putting down of the words seeming to bring my going home nearer.

'My dear Mrs Flannigan,

'I am happy to be able to tell you that I am delivered of premature twins, both small but thriving. My confinement was easy and I had the services of a physician. The babes are named Patrick and Gobnait which will please Dadda as they are the names of his own parents. As soon as the weather improves I hope to return for a visit to Ireland. I am more miserable than I ever was in my life before. Mr O'Hara, for all his Irish descent, is neither a loving nor a provident husband.'

I stopped, staring down at what I had written. I had not meant to betray my unhappiness so flagrantly. I had no desire to present myself as a misused wife for the family to pity. I screwed up the piece of paper and dropped it into the waste-paper basket, but there was no time to start a fresh sheet because Patrick had woken, wet and hungry, and was making his displeasure known.

It was evening by the time the babies were fed and changed and the apartment tidied up. At this season it was quite dark by teatime and I lit the lamps to cheer the high, gloomy rooms. Both the children slept peacefully, Gobnait with her tiny thumb stuck in her

131

mouth. I removed it, making a note to buy some bitter aloes, and could not avoid a wry smile for even the buying of a simple remedy meant careful counting of the little money that Chas grudgingly gave me.

There was a guinea in my purse and I had put a few silver coins in my linen drawer. Chas might filch a small coin from my purse but the guinea, whose loss would be immediately spotted, he would leave.

The coins were not there, though I clearly remembered putting them under the layers of washed and starched undergarments. I sat back on my heels and began to lift out each garment and shake it. There were no coins and, as I reached for the last item, I realised that something else was missing too. The lovely gold bracelet that Madame La Comtesse had given me was no longer there! I knew I had put it there, but at some time Chas must have found it. A slow and dangerous anger began to burn in me. The bracelet had been one of the few valuables that the Countess had managed to bring out of France and it had been a gift for my children. Lord knows but they would have little enough! Chas had stolen it, no doubt to pay a gambling debt, and I was more angry than I had been in my life before. I folded up the garments and put them back, and all the time my insides churned with rage and my ears were pricked for his step on the stair.

It came at last and I straightened up, smoothing down my hair, drawing a deep breath as if I were preparing to go into battle. This time I would not allow him to start complaining about my shortcomings and so avoid explaining his own behaviour.

He opened the door fumblingly and stood smiling at me in the foolish way that betrayed he had been drinking.

'You may take that expression off your face, my pretty little wife, for I won my bout tonight. I even won a silver cup—a silver-gilt to be strictly accurate!' he announced, placing it with flourish on the table.

'You've been boxing and drinking,' I began.

'In that order, my sweet!' He bowed and swayed slightly. 'I knocked out young Ramsey earlier and then we went off for a tiny celebration. Only a tiny celebration! Now you can't grudge me that.'

'I grudge you gold bracelets,' I said stonily.

'Gold bracelets? What in the world are you talking about?' He gave me another foolish grin. 'When did I have a gold bracelet?'

'Since you stole it from the drawer,' I accused. 'There were some coins there too and you took those as well!'

'I don't believe I have to account to you for what I take and don't take,' he began, but at that my temper spilled over.

'The countess gave me the bracelet for the baby. She brought it with her from France and it was one of the most expensive things I ever had! I knew you'd take it for your gambling and so I hid it away, and I was right to hide it away because you stole it anyway! You went through my drawer and you took it! To pay some gambling debt, I suppose, or is it now on some doxy's wrist? My God, Chas, you call me low Irish but there's nothing lower than a man who steals from his own children! You're useless, do you know that? Useless as a husband for you never gave me any pleasure, useless, useless!'

Once I had begun I couldn't stop. I could hear my own voice ranting on and on, and getting shriller and shriller, and all the time he stood there in the open doorway, swaying a little on his spindly legs, with a foolish grin on his broad, freckled face. I could hear voices below—the Pettifers must have heard the commotion, and one of the babes began to yell, disturbed by the noise I dare say. I was conscious of these things only as a background to my own rage.

I had picked up the silver-gilt cup and it was heavy in my hand. I am not certain exactly when I picked it up. I only knew it was heavy in my hand, and Chas swayed to and fro in a red mist that blotted out the rest of the room. I flung the cup. I remember the action of throwing but my aim went wide; it struck the edge of the door and bounced on to the landing and there was a clattering noise as it rolled to the bannister.

Everything happened then in slow motion. Chas took a step forward and then he crumpled up, blood pouring from his nose, a look of blank astonishment on his face that made me want to laugh. I think I did laugh, though I could feel tears pouring down my cheeks, and there was someone rushing up the stairs.

It was John Pettifer, his pleasant young face rigid with shock. I can remember that his wife was at his heels, that her face bore the same expression.

I can remember his voice cutting across my laughter, saying that Charles was dead. And for some reason I can never explain, I went on laughing harder then before.

CHAPTER EIGHT

The only death I could remember was my own mother's and then I had been very young and grieving. I was still young but I felt old. Dear Lord, but I felt much older than my actual age of eighteen, and I was not grieving. I couldn't even pretend to grieve for Charles O'Hara. All that I could feel was a dull sense of shock at the way in which he had died.

Mr Pettifer had run to fetch the physician and Mrs Pettifer had quietened the babies, and at some time during that endless night two constables had come to carry the body to the surgery. I sat by the fire, gulping some brandy that someone had poured, and people walked around me, talking in low voices. The countess came downstairs, her nose sharp with curiosity, but she was kind, folding an extra shawl about me and ordering one of the men who had come to scrub the floor clean of blood.

'There will have to be an inquest, Mrs O'Hara,' Mr Pettifer said, 'in order to determine the exact cause of death. You do understand, don't you?'

A couple of days had passed, days in which I fed the babies and changed them, and even ate meals that Mrs Pettifer carried up to me. She was a kind little woman and it troubles me that I never did thank her properly. It troubles me too that I felt so little. I had lived with Chas for nearly a year but his sudden going left no space in my life. I was even pleased when I woke at night to realise that I was alone in the wide bed and could stretch out without bumping my leg against a hunched and snoring figure.

'Inquest?' I looked up at him.

'The physician won't sign the death certificate until cause of death is established,' Mr Pettifer said again.

'I don't know what happened,' I said.

'That's something we will find out at the inquest,' he nodded. 'Unfortunately your presence will be required there, Mrs O'Hara.'

'And the funeral? That's tomorrow, isn't it?' I shook my head, feeling oddly disorientated.

'I took the liberty of making the arrangements. You said that I might. Mr Francis O'Hara will be attending. You told me to send word to him.'

'Yes. Yes, of course,' I shook my head again and he patted my hand in a shyly embarrassed fashion.

'You must try to bear up,' he said, and I thought ruefully that he didn't seem to know exactly what to say just as I didn't seem to know exactly how to behave.

At home there would have been a wake with candles burning at the head and feet of the corpse and the cabin full of neighbours reciting the virtues of the deceased. Here there were lowered voices and muted footsteps and the countess bringing down a black dress and cloak and a bonnet with a thick black veil.

'For it is fitting that a widow should look like a widow,' she told me. 'You must gain sympathy, my dear.'

I wondered why I needed to gain sympathy, but I couldn't find the interest to ask the question. I was still in a numbed, uncaring state and all I wanted was to be left alone.

The funeral was as bleak as I had imagined it would be. I had gone to the funeral parlour to see Chas and it was not like Chas at all. It was not like anybody at all. I stared down at

137

the lay figure in the open coffin and tried to feel pity for the young man whom I had married under false pretences, but I felt only a vague stirring of regret. I bent, to touch my lips to the cold forehead, and turned away, pulling the thick veil over my face.

Mrs Pettifer had stayed at home to care for the twins and the weather was too inclement to allow the countess to venture out, so it was on Mr Pettifer's arm that I leaned as we went down the aisle for the Requiem Mass. The church where Patrick and Gobnait had been baptised only three days before had the same flowers in the vases on the Lady Altar, and the words of the Mass had a poignant quality. Not until halfway through the service did I realise that Frank O'Hara was also in church.

Word of his brother's sudden death must have reached him scarcely a few hours after he had returned home. I glanced across at his set features and black suit, wondering if he had just arrived and had had no time to call upon me. He must have become conscious of my regard for he turned his head slightly and I felt a chill of uneasiness as I saw the blaze of hatred in his pale eyes. The service over we made our way slowly behind the hired pall-bearers to the graveside. I stood, my face veiled and my head bowed in the conventional posture of mourning and, all the time, I could feel that inimical gaze upon me. He turned and walked away as I was sprinkling a handful of earth on the coffin and when I looked up again he had gone. Again the uneasiness swept over me and, when I glanced at Mr Pettifer, I saw that his face was drawn and anxious.

'We must get you home quickly,' was all that he said as he drew my hand through his arm. 'It is a very brief time since you were confined and this shock on top of everything else might prove very harmful.'

'My brother-in-law never even spoke to me,' I said.

'Doubtless he is grieved and upset,' Mr Pettifer said. 'Let me help you up into the coach, my dear Mrs O'Hara. The wind is really very keen.'

A widow was treated like an invalid, I discovered. She was coddled and petted, given a brandy in lady-like nips, and tucked up with a hot stone at her feet. A widow who had just given birth to twins was treated twice as tenderly. The problem lay in me. I had regained my strength more quickly than any English lady would have done and I had plenty of milk though the countess had warned me it was likely to curdle because of the shock. The only shock I could sense in myself was a faint unreality as if I were encased in glass and nothing could come near enough to touch me.

'You must wear your veil down at the inquest, my dear,' the countess advised me, 'but when the coroner asks you his questions then you must put back the veil and show your

139

face, very pale, heavy-eyed.'

'I can't think why,' I said puzzled. 'Why do I have to make an impression?'

'To gain sympathy, perhaps?' She stood, her head a little on one side, regarding me.

'Why should I try to gain sympathy?' I asked in astonishment. 'The coroner will want to know what happened, won't he?'

'Yes, my dear.' The old lady tapped her stick on the floor, hesitated, and went away again without saying anything more.

Something was wrong. I could feel it all about me like a gathering mist and in that mist shapes moved, shapes I could neither recognise nor banish. The inquest had been set for two days after the funeral and Frank never came near to offer his sympathies. I hoped very much that he had gone home again, but when we reached the dingy little courtroom the first person I saw was Francis O'Hara, grim-faced and black suited, seated on the front row of high-backed benches.

I took my place at the other end of the bench and, mindful of the countess's advice, pulled my veil down and sat, my black-gloved hands clasped in my lap. The Pettifers took their places behind me and through the mist of unreality that surrounded me came a sudden question. Why was little Mrs Pettifer here and who was looking after the babies? I remembered then that Madame had come downstairs and offered to sit with them until the inquest was over. They were contented babies but the countess was elderly and I hoped these formalities would be quickly over so that I could get back to them.

The coroner wore an old-fashioned tie wig and a pair of gold-rimmed spectacles which he looked over rather than through. There was a clerk seated at one end of the long table and throughout the proceedings he scratched away busily with a pen that I longed for him to change.

Evidence of identification was given by the physician who looked, not at me nor at the coroner, but at a point somewhere above his head as if his recollections were printed on the air.

'You examined the body of the deceased,' the coroner was saying. 'Can you, in simple terminology, give us your findings?'

'The deceased was a young man of twenty-four, sturdily built. His death, as far as I could ascertain, was due to a massive haemorrhage from the brain cavity,' the physician said.

'Did you form any conclusions as to the cause of the haemorrhage?'

'I examined the skull of the deceased very minutely. There was a depression in the left frontal lobe, caused, I would say, by a severe blow to the temple. In plain terms the skull was fractured, sir.'

'I understand,' said the coroner, consulting some notes that lay before him, 'that you were summoned to the apartment of the deceased a week before the event we were investigating today?'

'I was called there to assist at the confinement of Mrs Charles O'Hara,' the physician said. 'The lady had gone into premature labour and was delivered, about twenty minutes after my arrival, of twins.'

'Surviving?'

'Yes, indeed. A healthy boy and girl. The delivery was quite straightforward.'

'And the mother?' The coroner glanced over his spectacles at me.

'A healthy young woman who recovered physically with remarkable rapidity,' the physician said.

'You say "physically"?' the coroner said.

'With a premature confinement there are often side-effects—delayed shock resulting sometimes in mental confusion and sometimes in a quite irrational dislike of the husband.'

'Were such symptoms present?' the coroner enquired.

'Mrs O'Hara did seem to be somewhat hostile towards her husband,' the physician said. 'He was not present at the birth and when he did arrive he was, I fear, somewhat discomposed—in his cups, which naturally angered Mrs O'Hara.'

I wondered what on earth any of this had to do with Chas dying. The coroner, having shuffled the papers in front of him, thanked the physician and requested Mr Pettifer to step up to the witness seat.

I found myself listening with an almost strained attention to Mr Pettifer, though the questions began innocently enough.

'You are a lawyer by profession, sir?'

'A law student. I have not yet taken my final Bar examinations.'

'And you reside in the apartments below Mr and Mrs O'Hara?'

'With my wife, yes.'

'Will you tell us exactly what happened on the night Mr O'Hara died?' the coroner invited.

'We had attended a small party there earlier—to celebrate the baptism of the twins,' Mr Pettifer began. 'We left just before supper, and I spent the even studying. I spend most evenings studying. At about midnight—I cannot swear as to the exact time—I heard voices from the upper landing. I came out to see what was amiss and I saw Mr O'Hara crumple to his knees and then fall.'

'Did he strike his head against anything as he fell?'

'No. He fell with his head on the carpet,' Mr Pettifer said. 'I ran upstairs at once and attempted to revive Mr O'Hara, but he had neither pulse nor heartbeat. There was a quantity of blood which apparently had issued from Mr O'Hara's nose. I saw almost at once that it was useless.'

'When you entered the room,' the coroner enquired, 'did you notice Mrs O'Hara?'

'She was standing there, looking very white and shocked,' Mr Pettifer said.

'You say that you heard voices.' The coroner leaned forward and stared intently at him. 'Did you see or hear anything else?'

'There was a cup, a silver goblet, had fallen against the bannister. I did just notice it, but I was naturally in a hurry to reach Mr O'Hara and render what assistance I could.'

'Mr Pettifer, as a student of the law you will appreciate the importance of exact and pertinent replies,' the coroner said. 'I want you to think very carefully indeed before you answer the next question. Did you see anyone drop or throw the goblet?'

I knew now where the questions were tending and all the unreality that had surrounded me was gone. I was suddenly terrified.

'My head was below the level of the bannister when the goblet came to rest,' Mr Pettifer said, slowly and carefully.

'Thank you.' The coroner nodded to the clerk who scratched away more excruciatingly than before.

My own name was being called. I put back my veil as the countess had instructed, and made my way to the chair, wondering why I should feel as if every eye was on me in accusation.

'Mrs O'Hara, were you on good terms with your husband?' The question was flung at me in such an unexpected fashion that I could not prevent an audible gasp.

'Yes?' The coroner adjusted his wig and gazed at me. Behind the gold-rimmed spectacles his eyes were cold pebbles.

'We were on good terms,' I said at last.

'Mrs O'Hara, I would advise you to think again,' he said sharply.

'We had arguments from time to time,' I said reluctantly.

'About what?'

'My husband left me alone a great deal,' I said.

'He had no profession, I understand?'

'None. I wanted him to take up some useful work but he preferred to waste his time in gambling.'

'My brother was a gentleman,' Frank O'Hara said loudly from where he sat. 'My brother was not trained for any occupation.'

'Mr O'Hara, you are not being questioned at this hearing,' the coroner said severely.

'I wanted him to work,' I repeated.

'And there were arguments between the two of you?' the coroner said, transferring his frown from Frank to me.

'Occasionally, but all married couples argue sometimes!' I exclaimed.

'Answer the question, Mrs O'Hara, and don't offer unsolicited comments!' he snapped.

145

There was no sympathy in his face for me, though I was certain I looked white and woebegone.

I swallowed nervously and fixed my eyes on his face.

'Did you and Mr O'Hara have one of these "arguments" on the night of his death?' he asked.

'Chas—Mr O'Hara went out that evening. I was accustomed to that.'

'At what hour did he return?'

'At about midnight. The babies had just gone off to sleep and he came home.'

'Did he tell you were he had been?'

'He'd won a boxing bout—that was what the cup was for—and then he'd been drinking with his friends.'

'Was he intoxicated?'

'No more than usual,' I said dryly.

'What did he say when he came in?'

'He told me he'd won the bout, and he showed me the cup.'

The questions were coming thick and fast now, and I could do nothing but answer truthfully.

'Showed you the cup, or gave it to you?'

'He—put it on the table, a small table by the door,' I said.

'Then how did it come to be lying on the landing near to the bannister?'

'I believed it rolled there,' I said.

'Rolled off the table and through the door,

146

past Mr O'Hara? You are an Irish woman, I understand?'

He had said 'woman' and not 'lady'. I nodded my head slowly.

'The Irish race is noted for the quickness of its temper,' the coroner observed, putting the tips of his fingers together and making a little arch of them, over which he peered.

I said nothing though I could feel my heart racing.

'Mrs O'Hara, is this your handwriting?' he asked abruptly.

He was holding a creased piece of paper in front of me. The words leapt and shimmered and blurred before my eyes.

'One of the constables who came to remove the body of your husband noticed it in the waste-paper basket and had the foresight to take it with him. Is it your writing, Mrs O'Hara?'

'I think—yes, yes, it is mine.'

'Written to a Mrs Flannigan, but not apparently signed.'

'Mrs Flanniagan is my old school-teacher,' I said. 'I started to write a letter to her.'

'Be so good as to read the last sentence,' he invited.

I took the paper but it shook so badly in my hand that the words danced crazily.

'Allow me to read it for you.' The coroner leaned and twitched it impatiently away from me. '"Mr O'Hara, for all his Irish descent, is

147

nether a loving nor a provident husband". Did you write those words, Mrs O'Hara?'

'I must have done.'

'Speak up, Mrs O'Hara! We cannot hear you properly.'

'I said I must have done it!' I repeated loudly.

'Mrs O'Hara, did you strike your husband with the silver cup which he brought home that evening?'

'No! No, I didn't strike him! I'm sure I didn't!'

'But you did throw it? You did fling it at him?'

'I didn't strike him!' I said loudly. 'I swear it never touched him!'

'Then you did throw it at him?'

'I threw it at the door. It hit the edge of the door,' I said desperately.

'Mrs O'Hara, you have just heard the expert testimony of the physician who stated that your husband expired from a massive brain haemorrhage, caused by a fracture of his skull! Skulls do not shatter by themselves, Mrs O'Hara! Bones do not break by themselves!'

In a moment he would be accusing me of murder. I knew it as surely as I knew there had been murder in my mind when I flung the cup. But it hadn't hit him. I could have sworn by all the saints that I didn't hit him.

The coroner paused, and I saw triumph in Frank O'Hara's face. No doubt Chas had confided that I was a virago. No doubt he believed me guilty of killing his brother. Perhaps, in his place, I would have felt the same.

I don't know what the next question would have been. It never came. Instead the door at the back of the court opened and Earl Sabre walked in.

He had that air of consequence which makes other men look unimportant. I feasted my eyes upon him, even forgetting for a moment the extreme danger in which I stood. He looked as cool and self-assured as if he were strolling into one of his clubs or into a drawing-room, and his lazy glance around even held a certain amusement.

'Sir?' The coroner stared at him, his eyebrows working furiously.

'Sir, I must apologise for coming so late,' Sabre said.

'Late? Are you on the list for those who are to give evidence in this enquiry?'

'No, sir, but fortunately I am able to bring it to a conclusion. Earl Sabre, sir, from Yorkshire. Mr Charles O'Hara was a friend of mine. Indeed I introduced him to his wife, though in recent months we had somewhat lost touch. My father was taken ill and died two months ago after a long sickness, and this is the first time I have had the opportunity of returning to London.'

'Have you evidence that will be of value in

this enquiry?' the coroner interrupted.

'I believe I have, sir. Do you wish me to take the oath?' Sabre enquired.

'This is an informal enquiry, but one naturally expects the truth to be told,' the coroner said pompously.

'Of course,' Sabre bowed again slightly.

'Perhaps you could give us the benefit of your knowledge?' the coroner murmured.

'Certainly. I must explain that I only learned of Chas's sudden death today when I visited White's. That is a club of which we are—were both members. I learned that he died with blood pouring from his nose.' Sabre paused.

'It has been established that Mr O'Hara died from a fractured skull,' the coroner informed him.

'I understand that he took part in a boxing contest in the earlier evening. A mutual acquaintance at White's told me so.'

'He won a silver cup in the bout,' Frank O'Hara put in.

'He was also knocked down twice,' Sabre said, 'before he succeeded in giving his opponent the *coup-de-grace*. Two severe blows to the head. The other man wanted him to retire, not merely because he craved the victory himself, but because, he told me, Chas seemed dazed. However, he apparently recovered sufficiently to adminster the knockout blow, as it is termed. Then he and a few of the others went to White's for some supper and a drink.'

'Several drinks, according to Mrs O'Hara,' the coroner interposed.

'Sir, may I be permitted to ask Mrs O'Hara a question?' Sabre enquired.

The coroner waved an assenting hand. In that court it was now Sabre who was the dominating figure and everyone else seemed to recognise and accept the fact.

'Mrs O'Hara.' Sabre turned to me, his voice politely formal. 'Mrs O'Hara, when Chas arrived home that night, in what state was he?'

'In his cups,' I said.

'Can you be more exact? Can you describe him?'

'He was swaying,' I said slowly. 'His eyes were slightly glazed and he spoke in a slurred kind of manner.'

'And you assumed he was in his cups.'

'Yes. Yes, I did.'

'Sir, I made some enquiries,' Sabre said, turning towards the coroner again. 'I asked some of those who had been with Chas that evening how much he had drunk. They assured me that he had drunk no more than a couple of glasses of champagne, far less than usual. That amount would not have caused any man, particularly a man accustomed to intoxicating liquor, to exhibit such symptoms as Chas displayed. His friends have told me that they themselves were surprised at the rapidity with which he seemed intoxicated.'

'Would they be willing to testify to that?' the coroner asked.

'I am certain they would. Indeed Mr Ramsey, who was the other competitor in the bout, expressed surprise that he had not been called,' Sabre said.

The coroner consulted his notes again though I suspected it was more to give himself time than anything else. When he looked up again he addressed himself to the physician who leaned forward in an attitude of keen attention.

'Doctor, would it be possible in your expert opinion for a man to recover from a severe blow to the head only to die of it a couple of hours later?'

'Certainly it would be possible,' came the prompt reply. 'In such a case the original injury would create a severe concussion with subsequent slow bleeding into the brain cavities. If the injured person were to lie down immediately in a darkened room with ice packs applied to the temples then the injury might be mitigated.'

'But Mr O'Hara went on to win his bout and then went to take supper with his friends before riding home,' Sabre said.

'That would certainly aggravate the problem considerably,' the physician said. 'Indeed, if the original injury were severe enough, death might result.'

'Chas was in the habit of boxing for exercise

and pleasure,' Sabre continued. 'He would have suffered blows to the head on numerous occasions. I suspect that the effect of repeated blows to the head might be cumulative, doctor?'

'Indeed it would.' The physician hesitated, then added, 'In my opinion the sport of boxing requires much stricter controls. There are frequently quite serious injuries reported as a result of this recreation.'

'Mr Sabre, we are most grateful to you for coming here today.' The coroner waved him to a seat. 'I would be grateful for the names and addresses of the gentlemen who were with Mr O'Hara during that evening, so that they may be questioned if necessary, but I am of the opinion, in view of this new testimony, that Mr O'Hara met his death as the result of an accidental blow to the head incurred during a friendly sparring match. Death by Misadventure is the verdict I therefore propose to record. You are all free to leave.'

He nodded towards me, still coldly. There was a certain regret in his voice as if he regretted the loss of an opportunity to arrest someone for murder.

'Mrs O'Hara, my condolences on your loss.'

Sabre had paused before me and was bowing gravely. I wanted him to put his arms round me and hold me against the shivering that gripped me, but having bowed he moved to the coroner and began talking to him, presumably giving him the names and addresses he had requested.

Frank O'Hara had risen and was staring at me with disappointed rage in his face. When he spoke his voice was thin with loathing.

'My brother should never have married you. As it is, may I make it clear that neither my father nor I consider that you or your children have any claim upon our sympathy or our generosity? There has been a miscarriage of justice here today. If it were not that I don't wish to cause my father more distress, I would take the whole matter further. As it is, the rent for your apartment will be paid up to the end of the month and after that I shall consider that you have no further claim on the estate.'

He turned on his heel and strode out before I had a chance to say anything. I adjusted my veil with shaking fingers and then Mr Pettifer offered me his arm, his pleasant face a mixture of relief and concern.

'Mrs O'Hara, I have a coach waiting so we may go home together,' he said, nodding towards where his wife stood.

'Yes, of course.' I made an effort to pull myself together. Sabre was still talking to the coroner and had apparently no intention of speaking to me again. It would have been foolish to wait for him.

I went out into the street where the coach waited, with Mr Pettifer escorting me as tenderly as if he expected me to collapse in a

154

heap on the pavement and Mrs Pettifer fluttering around me like a small anxious hen. Within the coach I sank back, closing my eyes, willing myself to stop shaking. I had been saved, I was aware, from a terrible danger, the danger of having been accused of killing my husband. If Sabre had not come—I shut my mind against the possibility and clasped my gloved hands tightly together.

I was free. That was the one good result of everything that had happened. I was, at eighteen, a widow with two beautiful children. In less than a month I would also be homeless, but before then surely some miracle would occur.

CHAPTER NINE

'My dear, I am so happy there has been a fortunate outcome,' the countess said. 'Mr Pettifer and I were exceedingly anxious as to what might transpire at the inquest. He being a lawyer knows only too well the pitfalls of circumstantial evidence.'

'He was beginning to believe that I had killed him,' I said, thinking of the coroner's hard, suspicious features and his sharp questions.

'It is his job to examine the facts,' Mr Pettifer said. 'Unfortunately facts can be interpreted in many ways. I am only too delighted that Mr Sabre was able to set the record straight.'

'You've both been very kind,' I said gratefully.

'You must put this sad episode behind you now,' the countess advised. 'Oh, if you had been driven to violence I do not believe that any of us would have blamed you! He was, I fear, a most unsatisfactory husband in many ways.'

'But young to die,' I said, wishing I could regret him more. In the few days since the inquest I had regained all my old vigour and energy and it was impossible to appear, even to myself, as a grieving widow.

'We all have our time to go,' the countess remarked. 'I myself cannot mourn too deeply for a man who steals his own children's possession!'

'I am sorry about the bracelet, Madam,' I said.

'Perhaps it is fortunate that the matter of the bracelet was not raised at the inquest,' Mr Pettifer said, rising to take his leave. 'It provided you with such a strong motive that the coroner might not have allowed Mr Sabre's evidence to weigh so heavily. You know, Mrs O'Hara, that your children are in law entitled to some share in any estate your husband might have had. If you wish me to look into the matter for you I shall only be too happy.'

'I want nothing from the O'Hara's,' I said flatly. 'I shall rear my children without their help.'

'That must be your decision, of course.' He bowed, looking slightly disappointed at the prospect of losing his first brief, and went to the door. The countess, who had been standing by the window looking out into the street, turned to follow him, her sharp old eyes alight with sudden mischief as she informed me.

'Mr Sabre seems to be in the act of alighting at the front door, my dear. I assume he is coming to pay his official condolences.'

I had not expected ever to see him again. Having done his duty by telling what he had learned of the circumstances that surrounded his old friend's death, he could have ridden north with a clear conscience, forgetting that I existed. His coming was something I had ceased to hope for, and I stared at the countess in silence.

'Shall I ask him to step up, Mrs O'Hara?' Mr Pettifer, still eager to be of help, enquired.

'If you would be so kind,' I said numbly.

'Lend me your arm, Mr Pettifer.' The countess tapped her way towards him. 'One really ought not to intrude at such a moment. I understand that he and Mr O'Hara were close friends.'

Her voice and expression were completely

157

innocent, but I could see the mischievous speculation at the back of her eyes. I wondered how much she had guessed the link between Sabre and me.

Sabre and me! It was the first time for months that I had dared to couple our names in my own mind. I stood for a moment, irresolute, as the countess and Mr Pettifer went out, and then I found myself hurrying round, frantically plumping up cushions, poking the fire into a blaze, hesitating before the mirror to stare at my flushed face above the high collar of my black dress. When he had seen me in the courtroom I had looked white and terrified, as guilty as if I had really committed a murder. It was no wonder that he had not come to talk to me or visited me since.

I had no time even to comb my hair before his knock sounded at the door. I drew a deep breath and opened it, my voice pitched at what I hoped was a pleasant conversational level.

'Mr Sabre, good-day to you! Won't you please come in?'

'I trust I'm not intruding at a difficult time,' he bowed. 'Mr Pettifer tells me you are receiving company.'

'Please come in.' I held the door wider, stepping aside to allow him to pass. I was quite certain that the countess had stopped on the way to her own rooms to listen on the staircase.

Sabre walked in, closed the door firmly, and

seated himself in one of the two high-backed chairs without waiting to be asked. His expression as he looked up at me reminded me of the countess. There was the same knowing mischief at the back of his eyes.

'How are you, Sabre?' I asked nervously, taking the chair opposite him. 'I'm very pleased you called because it gives me the opportunity to thank you very much for your help at the inquest.'

'Fausty, you can drop the pretence,' he said bluntly. 'You can trust me to keep your secrets.'

'Secrets? I don't have secrets,' I began, but he shook his head at me in a reproving fashion.

'I think you have lots of secrets, Fausty dear. Those premature twins I heard mentioned— now you never breathed a word to me about being pregnant when I was here last.'

'It was none of your business,' I said.

'You should have invited me to be godfather,' he remarked, leaning back and crossing one leg over the other. 'You could have counted on me for a handsome present. Where are they?'

'The babies are asleep in the bedroom,' I said.

'You don't mind if I have a peep at them, do you?' he enquired, beginning to rise. 'Like most bachelors I'm very fond of small babies.'

'They're just babies,' I said quickly, but he

was already moving with a deceptively lazy stride to the inner room, and there was nothing I could do but trail at his heels and watch helplessly as he stooped over the two drawers in which they lay, tiny heads russet against the white sheets.

When he straightened up again his expression had changed, the amusement being placed by a hard, wary look.

'What are they called?' he asked.

'Patrick and Gobnait,' I said in a small voice.

'They're a handsome pair,' he said.

'They're very good babies. They only wake up when they are wet and hungry.' I was speaking too quickly and my voice was too high.

Sabre's grey eyes were steely as they met mine.

'I'm their father,' he said. It was not a question, nor an accusation, but a calm statement of fact.

Even if I'd wanted to deny it it would have been useless. Twin miniatures of him lay there and there was no way they could be denied. I stood there, feeling rather like a small girl about to be scolded for some misdemeanour.

'So you married Chas with my babes in you.' His tone was slow and reflective.

I turned and walked back into the other room where, after a moment, he followed me, taking two glasses from the sideboard and pouring us the last of a bottle of negus that stood there. When he handed one to me I began to shake my head, but he looked so stern that I hastily changed my mind and meekly accepted it.

'So you married Chas when you were pregnant by me,' he said again. 'Did Chas guess?'

'I'm not sure.' I took a gulp of the negus and found it warming.

'Chas was not a complete fool! He must have suspected!'

'Suspected, I think. He had begun to ask questions.'

'And died most conveniently before he received the answers.'

'Mother of Mercy, but you're starting to sound like the coroner!' I exclaimed. 'He was quite sure I'd hit Chas on the head with that silver cup!'

'And did you?' Sabre asked with interest.

'I missed,' I admitted and felt an unwilling grin spread across my face. 'The cup hit the edge of the door and then Chas fell down. He must have died of the injury he got in the boxing bout, exactly as you thought.'

'Poor old Chas!' Sabre tossed back his drink and set down the glass.

'He wasn't so wonderful!' I said indignantly. 'He drank quite heavily, you know, and he never gave me sufficient money for the housekeeping!'

'But you married him,' Sabre pointed out.

'What was I supposed to do?' I demanded. 'I was pregnant, Sabre! Dear God, but I had no wish to be disgraced!'

'You could have told me,' he said mildly.

'You'd gone north. You'd told me I ought to marry Chas. What else was I supposed to do?'

'You could have married me,' he said.

'You made it very clear that I wasn't good enough for your fine family,' I said resentfully. 'You told me your father would cut you out of his will if you married someone who wasn't what you call a lady. Oh, you made it very clear that I was good enough to tumble in the park or take to bed on an afternoon when you'd nothing better to do, but you pushed me on to Chas when it came to wedding bells!'

'Fausty, do you think I would have turned my back and walked away from you if I'd known you were carrying my child?' he asked reproachfully.

I put down the empty glass and twined my fingers in the silk of my dress. In a subtle way he was twisting everything about, making it seem that I was the one in the wrong.

'What are you going to do?' he asked.

I rose and walked over to the window. The rain had stopped and a feeble sunlight was drying up the puddles in the street below.

'I thought I would go home,' I said.

'To Ireland? Yes, you could do that,' he said.

'What else is there?' I asked. 'I've no money and this apartment is only rented to the end of the month. Anyway I'm homesick! I do have a family in Ireland, you know!'

'You could come north,' he said.

'Thank you, but I made one mistake when I let you seduce me,' I said bitterly. 'I'll not make another by becoming your mistress.'

'Fausty, I'm asking you to become my wife!' he exclaimed, coming to where I stood and turning me to face him.

'Why?' I asked bluntly. 'I'm still not quite a lady, you know.'

'My father died two months ago,' Sabre said. 'Sabre Hall and the mill are mine now. Nobody can disinherit me! I tell you frankly that if you'd told me you were with child I'd have wed you and let the consequences go hang! But now my father is dead and nobody can take my inheritance away. I can share it with you, Fausty. Don't you know that I love you? Don't you know that I went away loving you, that when I came back and found you'd taken my suggestion and married Chas I was more miserable than I've ever been in my life?'

'You hid it well,' I said dryly.

'Because I believed that you and Chas might have a chance together to be happy,' he said. 'You made it very clear that you didn't want me to stay, that I was intruding into your life. Was that because you didn't want me to know that you were with child?'

163

'I feared you'd guess the truth,' I said.

'Fausty, what fools we've both been!' he exclaimed. 'I thought that you didn't love me and you thought that I wouldn't marry you even to give my own offspring a name!'

It hadn't been exactly like that, I thought in confusion. Sabre had refused me in the first place, a fact he appeared to have forgotten. But I was past trying to make sense of it. I was past even wanting to work everything out logically. All that mattered was that I stood within the circle of his arms again and that he was kissing me.

'Marry me and come back with me to Sabre Hall,' he was pleading, and I felt a thrill of power because the rich and handsome Sabre had stooped to beg.

'It's too soon,' I began feebly.

'Darling, where is the sense in waiting out the customary year?' he demanded. 'Where would you go in the meantime? Back to Ireland to live with your family? There would be the width of the sea between us! Could you really endure that?'

I was silent, seeing in my mind's eye the cabin with Bridie trying to keep the taties hot for when Dadda came weaving home. I could see the twins, squabbling as they got under everybody's feet, and the road churned up into mud when the rain teemed down. I tried to picture myself, returning as a young widow with my two fatherless babes, and the love and pity that would surround me. And I knew that I loved the memory of home more than the reality. I loved the scent of peat and the sight of the golden gleams of sun that struck through the mist, but I had grown past that now. I could no longer live in a muddle even if it was a loving one. I was used to soft beds and a variety of foods. I was used to riding in a coach when I wanted to go any distance at all and to having a selection of dresses to wear. I suppose, by London standards, I lived very modestly, but by the standards I had grown up with I lived in luxury.

'Fausty!' Sabre gave me a slight shake. 'I'm twenty-six years old and until now I've never wanted to settle with one woman! I've never really wanted to settle in one place, but my father's dead now and I've the responsibilities of the estate to tie me in the north. I need someone to share that burden with me, and who could be better than the mother of my children?'

'Legally they're O'Hara children,' I said.

'If I were to marry you at once and then legally adopt them they would be entitled to bear my name,' he pointed out. 'All my family and friends need know is that I married you some time ago in London. They will assume we were wed before the babies were born and that I kept the marriage secret because I didn't want to quarrel with my father.'

'Why not simply say that you married a

widow with two small children?'

'Because even my Aunt Dotty who is exceedingly short-sighted will notice how like me they are.'

He was right and it was the sensible course of action but it meant we would be starting our married life together with a lie. That troubled me but Sabre was kissing me again and, after the months of pregnancy and the strain of trying to live on friendly terms with a husband I could not even respect, it was sheer bliss to know myself wanted.

'We'll be married at the end of the week,' he said, 'and I'll have the adoption formalities put in hand at once. You won't wear black at the ceremony, will you, my dear?'

'No, of course not.'

To wear mourning would be like having Chas as an invisible guest, I thought.

'My family will be puzzled that I married again so soon.'

'You're an adult, Fausty. You can marry where and when you have a mind.'

I suppose I could have reminded him that he too could have wed when he chose and risked his father's displeasure, but he spoke with such calm authority that I merely nodded and said with unusual meekness, 'I will wait a few months before I write to them.'

'You're not insisting on a honeymoon trip to Ireland then?' he said teasingly.

I shook my head. One day I would go back

and see them all again but the past year had created a chasm between my old life and the new one that stretched ahead. At the prospect of that new life my heart beat faster with a mixture of excitement and apprehension.

'Tell me about your family,' I said, 'I know so little about them. You mentioned an Aunt Dotty.'

'Short for Dorothy,' he told me. 'She and Aunt Sassie, short for Sarah, were my father's elder sisters. They've neither of them ever married but they more or less brought my father up. His own father made his fortune in the East India Company and had the sense to invest it in wool.'

'And was annoyed because he never received an honour from the Crown.'

'Furious is the word I would have chosen,' Sabre said with a grin. 'It was entirely due to him that I was saddled with a Christian name which I refuse to use!'

'He's dead now, is he?' I asked.

'He died when I was a boy,' Sabre said.

'And your mother?'

'When I was born. Sweetheart, why all the questions?' He tilted up my chin and looked down at me.

'Because your family will become my family now,' I told him.

'You're marrying me, not my family,' he interrupted. 'Wait until we get up into Yorkshire and you'll meet my Aunts Dotty and

167

Sassie soon enough. They've been at me for years to take a wife so they'll welcome you.'

Unspoken were the words 'even if you are an Irish nobody', but I felt them all the same.

'And the house? What is the house like?' I persisted.

'Wait and see.' There was teasing in his grey eyes again and then he bent his head and kissed me long and deep and I would have gone with him anywhere in the world at that moment without question.

'The priest will be a little shocked to be marrying me to another husband so soon after he read the funeral service over my first one,' I said, when I could catch my breath.

'Priest?' Sabre held me away from him and frowned slightly. 'Fausty, I love you very much but I'm damned if I'll marry you in a Papish ceremony. We'll have a good sound Anglican marriage.'

'Which would be no marriage at all,' I broke in.

'Perhaps not in the eyes of your church, but the wedding would be legal.'

'My Dadda would be horrified.'

'Your father's in Ireland and so are all the rest of the family. I've told you before, Fausty, that you're a grown woman now.'

'But I'm a good Catholic,' I argued.

'Darling, I wouldn't dream of interfering with your beliefs,' he said patiently. 'After we're wed you can practise your faith and nobody will stop you, but we'll have an Anglican marriage and my children will be reared as Anglicans.'

'Your children!' I began indignantly.

'Patrick Sabre and Gobnait Sabre,' he said, and dared me to contradict him.

I could have refused at that moment, I suppose, but I was not sure how much Sabre really wanted to marry me, nor what on earth I would do if at the last instant he changed his mind, refusing to take me or the children.

'Darling, is it so important to you?' he asked coaxingly. 'I never thought of you as a praying woman! And children ought to be brought up in the religion of their father.'

'Very well.' Again I found myself meekly agreeing, but there was resentment deep inside me all the same at the way he insisted on taking me on his own terms. I didn't want to examine my resentment too closely because I loved Sabre but I wished very much that I could afford to be proud.

'You've had a hard time these past weeks,' he said, gentle now that he had his way. 'Now it's my turn to take care of you, Fausty girl, and to give those children of ours the right start in life. You want that for them, don't you?'

I wanted everything for them, I realised, and I wanted even more for myself. I wanted to marry the man I loved and live on a fine estate and, at that moment, it seemed to me that a

169

Protestant ceremony was a small price to pay.

CHAPTER TEN

Sabre insisted on buying me a new gown for the wedding ceremony and I presented no very forceful argument. The new dress was the symbol of a new beginning. It was also very becoming, the narrow skirt and shoulder-puffed sleeves of a creamy velvet patterned in blue, the bodice of ruffled lace and the small velvet bonnet tied with blue ribbons.

The ceremony itself struck me as brief and cold, with no soaring Latin phrases to give meaning to the whole. I clutched a bunch of delicate snowdrops so tightly their stems must have been bruised, and only Mr and Mrs Pettifer were there to witness the event, Madame having remained behind to take care of the twins. Sabre had already begun the formal process of adoption.

'There is no need for either of them to know that they were adopted after our wedding,' he told me.

'What about your aunts?'

'As far as they, and everybody else is concerned, you and I were secretly married a year ago,' he said.

'Start something with a lie and it will end badly' was one of Dadda's favourite sayings. I pushed it out of my mind and nodded agreement. Sabre was the father of my children and the white lie would save them embarrassment in later life. Already poor Charles O'Hara was becoming a dim figure in my mind and it was hard to realise that I had ever been married to him.

There was no wedding breakfast such as I had had before. My trunk was packed, the keys of the apartment entrusted to John Pettifer for eventual return to the landlord, and we only had a celebration glass of champagne before we mounted the step up to the hired coach that would take us the three-day journey up to Yorkshire.

I had not realised before how very hard it is to travel with small babes, even when for most of the time they were rocked asleep by the motion of the coach. They still required to be fed and changed and, though the inns at which we stayed were very decent ones, I would have been exhausted long before we crossed into Yorkshire had it not been for Sabre's help. He displayed a side of his nature that I would not have dreamed existed in a man who was so cool and masculine. He sat for hours in the swaying coach holding one or other of the children with no sign of tiredness or impatience and when we stopped overnight along the way he was the one who got up and soothed Gobnait back to sleep when she woke crying.

'They are both pure Sabre, every inch of them!' he exclaimed. 'Nobody could mistake them for anyone's children but mine!'

'They're mine too,' I said mildly and he laughed, kissing my cheek as he answered.

'You gave birth to them for me, darling. For that I owe you an everlasting debt of gratitude!'

I didn't want his gratitude. I wanted him to make love to me but he was too taken up with the babies to spare time from admiring them and I reminded myself that there was the rest of our lives ahead of us. The novelty of the twins would wear off in time and we would grow into a loving closeness.

We reached Yorkshire at last and I looked eagerly out of the coach windows, anxious to see the country that was to be my new home. The roads were steeper and narrower here, the land falling away as we rose higher into the folds of grey-green grass, criss-crossed by brownish streams. Overhead the clouds scudded across the blue sky and there were glints of gold from the opening spring flowers that dotted the moor. There were no hedges such as I had seen in the south, but low stone walls curved the landscape and the few trees were twisted into grotesque shapes by the wind I could hear sweeping down the heights. There seemed to be very few houses apart from the occasional glimpse of a farmhouse in the distance and a row of cottages past which we rattled too fast for me to see them properly.

'We'll be there soon,' Sabre said, breaking a long silence.

I sat up, pulling my cloak about myself and wishing I had a mirror so that I could tidy my thick dark hair which was escaping from the net in which I had confined it. After three days travelling I felt tired and grubby but at least we would soon be home. The word 'home' had a comforting, familiar ring. I smiled at Sabre but he was adjusting the shawl about Patrick and didn't look up.

We were on level ground and I saw a row of cottages and a tall, gaunt building with a long wooden shed at its side.

'Is that the mill?' I asked eagerly. 'Is Sabre Hall near?'

'A mile beyond,' he said.

I was not sure exactly what to expect. The only estate I could imagine was a gracious house hidden behind high gates in a charming garden.

We began to climb as the road sloped upwards past the short grass that shrouded the landscape, past thorn bushes that clung to the meagre soil, past a narrow river that splashed down over boulders to a hump-backed bridge at the bottom of the hill. I could hear the screaming of the wind more plainly now and the horses' hooves tended to slip on the cobbles as they laboured upward.

'This is Sabre Hall,' Sabre said, and it was

impossible to tell if his mood was pleased or not.

There were no wrought iron gates or ordered lawns and flower beds. There was only an expanse of rough turf and beyond that the square, uncompromising bulk of a grey house.

I have tried since to recapture my first impression of Sabre Hall as I first saw it on that blustery afternoon. The only word that comes into my mind is 'brutal'. It was a brutal building, the stone walls unembellished by creepers, the square windows staring emptily, the high roof of dark tiles. It was a house without grace or softness and my heart sank as the coach drew up before a door of solid oak, set deep within the overhanging stone porch.

Sabre had opened the coach door and leapt down with Patrick in his arms as soon as we stopped. Through the window I saw the house door open and a small elderly woman, her grey hair clustering in ringlets about her face, hurried forward to meet him.

'Come and see my son and heir!' he exclaimed, putting the baby in her arms.

I felt what I can only describe as a pang of jealousy. The woman was holding Patrick with the slightly awkward tenderness of someone unused to children and it was a full minute before Sabre came back, leaning into the coach to take Gobnait from me.

'I must show my daughter to Aunt Sassie too,' he said.

No word about introducing his wife! I climbed down unaided and stood, a trifle forlornly, waiting to be noticed. Sabre had taken Patrick back and Aunt Sassie was holding Gobnait, peering into the tiny face and making little cooing noises. The two of them, aunt and nephew, were immersed in the babies. I gave a small cough and Aunt Sassie raised a rosy face and looked at me in an enquiring manner as if she were not certain exactly who I was.

'Aunt Sassie, this is my wife, Faustina,' Sabre said in a belated manner.

'Faustina.' Under its fringe of grey curls her face was round as an apple, tiny blue eyes appraising me.

'Shall we go in before the babies catch cold?' Sabre was enquiring.

It was certainly cold, the wind keen as a knife as it cut around the corner of the house. A thickset man in breeches and gaiters had arrived and was talking to the coachman.

We went through the main door into a long stone-floored hall with doors to left and right and three arched windows at the back that gave the apartment the aspect of a church. There were some sheepskin rugs on the floor and a small fire burned in a wide hearth set between two of the doors. From one of them came a plump woman whose white apron and cap proclaimed her status as housekeeper. She was talking rapidly, her accent so pronounced that I couldn't follow the words. The babies were handed over to her and I trailed after Sabre and Aunt Sassie into a large, handsome drawing-room with velvet curtains hanging at the windows and a much brighter fire burning in the hearth. The furniture was elaborately carved and polished and I wondered if the plump woman kept it clean and shining.

'Aunt Sassie asked you to sit down,' Sabre said. There was a faint note of reproach in his voice and I blushed, realising that I was staring round like a zany, and sat down hastily on an over-stuffed chair, loosening the strings of my bonnet.

'Mary will bring us some tea,' Aunt Sassie said. 'Sabre, what possessed you to wait so long before telling us that you were married? Your letter came as a very great shock!'

'I could hardly have made my marriage public while father was alive,' Sabre said.

'But at the funeral—?'

'At the funeral I was not in the humour to announce good news when everyone was so upset,' he interrupted.

'But it would have mitigated our grief to learn that you had two beautiful children,' his aunt said. 'You know how much your dear father wished for grandchildren!'

'But only from the right wife,' Sabre said.

'Oh, he would not have approved of you marrying an Irishwoman,' she agreed. 'We had the most dreadful trouble with those Irish weavers we brought in during the Luddite riots. Lazy to the marrow! No, he would never have approved of an Irishwoman.'

She smiled and twinkled at him, nodding her curly grey head, behaving as if I were not even in the room. I felt my cheeks begin to burn again, this time with indignation, not shame.

A maidservant—Mary, I supposed—came in with a pot of tea on a silver tray and Aunt Sassie leaned to pour it out into three delicate fluted cups. The china was so fine I could see the light through it and the liquid so scaldingly black that I could only sip it cautiously.

'So! you are wed!' Aunt Sassie leaned back and twinkled at Sabre.

'And prepared to settle down and buckle to, as father would say,' he said, making a grimace.

'I am happy to hear it,' she said primly.

'Is that the housekeeper, the woman who took the twins?' I broke in.

'That's Huldah,' Sabre said. 'She's been here for years.'

'She'll take excellent care of the dear babes,' Aunt Sassie said. 'Your news certainly pleased her, my dear boy. You know how much she likes looking after young ones.'

'Huldah is immortal,' Sabre said.

'I haven't met your other aunt yet,' I said, determined not to be ignored.

'My sister, Dorothy, is very much of an

invalid,' Aunt Sassie said.

'I have four sisters,' I began, but she was talking to Sabre again, her eyes sliding away from me.

'You must talk to Oldfield, Sabre. He is getting extremely stubborn in his old age, but in view of his long service it would be most unjust to turn him off: Perhaps we could employ a younger man to do the real work and retain Oldfield as supervisor?'

'I'll talk to him.' Sabre drank his boiling tea as easily as if it were lukewarm.

'The babies will require feeding,' I put in.

'I'm glad you reminded me!' Aunt Sassie gave me her rosy smile. 'Sabre, you remember Maggie Ackroyd, Maggie Baxter that was? She lost her own babe a couple of days since— nothing infectious; the poor babe was very puny from the start, but Maggie has plenty of milk and she's a clean, healthy girl.'

'So you've employed her as a wet nurse!' Sabre exclaimed. 'Aunt Sassie, you're a marvel!'

'I've installed her in the nursery—your old nursery,' she continued. 'Her husband's gone down to Leeds for six months to work at his uncle's shop, so she'd have been all alone in her cottage anyway.'

'I feed Patrick and Gobnait myself,' I said loudly.

'Darling, there's no need for you to be tied down to that now that we have Maggie,' Sabre said, looking faintly amused as he handed over his cup for more tea.

'But I'm quite capable of feeding them myself,' I argued.

'They probably do it in Ireland,' Aunt Sassie murmured, her tone suggesting Darkest Africa.

'Ladies don't usually feed their own children,' Sabre said to me kindly. 'The workers' wives do, of course, but if it's at all possible ladies foster their babies.'

I wanted to cry that Patrick and Gobnait were my children and I would nourish them myself, but having explained the point of etiquette to me Sabre had turned back to his aunt and the latter, shooting me one of her twinkling glances, said, 'Would you like to explore a little, Faustina? Huldah will tell you the way around the house and you'll want to change for supper.'

I had pictured Sabre, his arm about my waist, leading me from room to room, showing me the places where he had played as a child, the cupboard where he kept his fishing rod, his schoolbooks. Instead I found myself putting down my cup and rising to walk with as much dignity as I could muster to the door. Sabre smiled at me, but almost at once his gaze returned to Aunt Sassie and as I went through the door the two of them were deep in conversation again.

I closed the door softly, resisting a childish

impulse to slam it, and stood for a moment in the empty, echoing hall. Opposite the drawing-room where we had been sitting, a half-open door led into a dining-room. There was a massive sideboard against one wall and over the high mantelshelf the portrait of a fierce old gentleman, his greying red hair tied back in a queue. That was obviously Sabre's formidable grandfather and I went over to stare up at the handsome, implacable old face, remembering what Sabre had told me about him.

'He made his fortune in the East India Company and sank the profits into wool. He bought up most of the valley and built Sabre Hall to overlook his mill and his cottages, but he never got over the fact he was never offered a title. It soured him and he died an embittered man.'

The mouth was harsh and the eyes disapproved of me. I forced myself to meet his gaze, reminding myself that he was dead and I was alive but, under that piercing regard, I could feel myself shrinking down into an Irish peasant again.

An inner door opened and the housekeeper came in, stopping short as she noticed me standing there.

'You are Huldah,' I said pleasantly, turning to smile at her.

'Happen I am,' she said unsmilingly.

'I am Faustina, Sabre's wife.' I kept my tone cordial and inclined my head as she dipped into a shallow, grudging curtsey.

'I heard t'master's taken a wife,' Huldah observed. 'Well, tha's a bonnie lass an'all, but t'owd master'll whirl on's grave to think of an Irishwoman here.'

She sounded gloomily satisfied like a prophetess whose worse fears have just come true. I could feel my good-humour ebbing away fast but I restrained myself.

'I'm here on the way up to our room, but the picture attracted my attention,' I said, wondering why I was bothering to explain my actions.

'T'owd master,' Huldah observed, looking up at it. 'He'd not stand for any nonsense!'

'Is that Sabre's father?' I asked in surprise. 'I took it to be his grandfather.'

'That's t'other owd master,' Huldah said. 'His picture's up in't gallery, he were t'one built t'house.'

'So that was Sabre's father,' I mused, and could understand why Sabre had not dared to defy him openly.

'Were tha wanting something?' Huldah asked.

I would have liked to go through the inner door to where I guessed the kitchens were, but I guessed that she would regard it as an intrusion. There would be time later for me to explore the back premises.

'Perhaps you could show me to our bedchamber,' I suggested.

'Up the stairs on the right and down to the end of the Long Gallery,' said a decided feminine voice from the door.

I turned as a tall, thin woman of indeterminate age paused on the threshold.

This was clearly Aunt Dotty. She looked like a pulled thin version of Aunt Sassie, her grey curls fluffed out round a vast turban of pink and purple, her face a long pink rectangle with spectacles perched at the end of her bony nose. She didn't look very delicate and the grip of her knotted fingers was punishingly firm.

'I thought tha was resting,' Huldah began, a note of scolding in her voice.

'Time enough to rest when I am in my grave,' the other said briskly. 'Come along, girl, and I'll show you the way upstairs.'

She jerked her turbaned head at me and I followed her meekly out into the hall again, down to the further door which she pushed open to reveal a small lobby out of which stairs, polished and carpeted in dull red, rose up.

'Father disliked what he called "grand stairways",' she observed over her shoulder as she preceded me. 'He disliked wasting anything, even space. I'm Aunt Dotty by the way. Baptised Dorothy but known as Dotty since I could toddle. This is the Long Gallery and the main bedchamber is at the end, though I cannot imagine why a complete stranger should wish to see it.'

'I'm Sabre's wife,' I said in bewilderment. 'I'm sorry but I thought you knew.'

'So you're the Irish biddy,' she said, pausing on the step to look down at me. 'I did wonder why you were strolling about here but if you're wed to Sabre that explains a lot. Maggie Ackroyd is feeding two babies in the nursery. Are they yours?'

'Patrick and Gobnait,' I said.

'I didn't look too closely,' Aunt Dotty said. 'I don't like babies much. Puppies are more amusing and less trouble to rear. What's the matter?'

'The gallery,' I said, awed as I gazed down the panelled chamber that ran the entire length of the house. 'It's beautiful!'

'Hammerbeam roof and all these windows let in the light,' Aunt Dotty nodded. 'My father loved the gallery. It was the only thing he and I had in common. For the rest we never ceased quarrelling. He would have it that I was unfit to marry on account of being mad.'

'Oh, but surely not!' I protested.

'Oh, he was partly right,' Aunt Dotty informed me cheerfully. 'I am exceedingly mad from time to time. Today is one of my better days else I should be locked up. But being mad is no bar to wedlock in my opinion. If he'd let some man marry me I might have turned out sane. That's his portrait there. Sometimes, when I'm feeling particularly spiteful, I turn his face to the wall. That's your room at the

183

end there.'

She turned, her bunched skirts flying, and loped back towards the head of the staircase, leaving me in a considerable state of agitation. I turned to the portrait and found myself staring at a white-wigged Sabre, the mouth a slash, the eyes grey steel. This then was the man who had built the house and settled his family here. The man in the dining-room portrait had been his son. That had been a peppery face but I quailed even more before the icy ruthlessness in this one's expression.

His was the only picture in the gallery though there were spaces for more. It was as if he would tolerate no other presence.

A door on my right stood ajar and, through it, I heard a woman begin to sing. The voice was sweet and high, raised in a melody that was unfamiliar to me. I pushed the door wider and walked into a lobby off which three doors opened. The one on the left was open and in the wide bedchamber beyond a young woman was holding one of the babies against her shoulder, patting the shawled back to bring up the wind. When she saw me she made to rise, her song dying away, but I shook my head hastily.

'Please don't get up! You must be Maggie Ackroyd.'

'Yes'm.' She gave a small, shy smile.

'It's very good of you,' I said awkwardly, 'to nurse my children.'

'No bother,' she said, in the flat, rapid accent I was beginning to follow more easily as my ear grew accustomed to it. 'I lost my own bairn and I've milk to spare.'

'Their names are Patrick and Gobnait,' I said.

'Irish names?' She looked slightly surprised.

'They are half-Irish,' I told her, and felt as if I were trying to lay claim to some part of them.

Her eyes, wide-set in a rosy face, moved from me to where the other twin lay in a carved cradle.

'They'm Sabre bairns,' she said, and resumed her soft, wordless song.

I went out into the gallery again, telling myself firmly that it was a good thing she was clearly prepared to be fond of them. She smelt clean and fresh too and she was young. My babes would be in good hands. But my own breasts were beginning to ache with their fullness of milk, and my loneliness was increasing.

I walked on, past two closed doors, and entered the room Aunt Dotty had indicated. It was a vast, high-ceilinged chamber, hung in a bronze velvet that gleamed dull gold where it caught the firelight.

My trunk had been brought up and placed on a carved bench at the foot of the wide bed. I found myself looking at that bed with its pillows humped beneath a bronze quilt and wondering uneasily if Sabre's father or grandfather had died in it. I have never had the second sight but there was a brooding presence in that room that weighed upon my spirits.

I went to one of the long windows that overlooked the valley and opened the casement wide. The air that rushed in was so cold and sharp that it made me gasp for breath. The soft rains of Ireland and the gentle green of her round hills seemed further away than they had ever been. From my vantage point I could see the tough crisp turf sloping to the cobbled road that wound its way down to the bridge across the river. I could see the dark bulk of the mill and figures, small as ants, moving about in the fenced yard. At the other side of the valley the land rose up into a sombre moor, criss-crossed by streams and stone walls. From this distance I couldn't see the tiny golden flowers and, with the approach of the evening, the sky had darkened, clouds rolling in and the first piercing drops of rain falling on my hand when I rested it on the window ledge.

My breasts felt huge and swollen. I would have to pad them lest they begin to leak during the evening. It was so foolish that I should be forced to suffer discomfort while another woman fed my babies. But they were Sabre babies now and, for better or worse, I was a Sabre wife.

I was, I told myself firmly, the new mistress

of Sabre Hall. Free from the noisy, cramped cabin where my brothers and sisters tumbled. Freed from Chas O'Hara with his spindly legs and his gambling. Freed from the threat of poverty. I kept telling myself that as I unpacked my gowns and I told myself too, very firmly, that the tears were gathering in my eyes only because my breasts were so sore.

CHAPTER ELEVEN

'My dear Mrs Flannigan,

'I hope my recent silence has not made you or any of my family anxious, so much has happened that I have had little leisure to write. I trust you received my brief note, telling you of the death of my husband, Charles O'Hara. I was much exercised in my mind as to whether or not to return to Ireland but I was offered matrimony by another gentleman and, though the speed of my remarriage may seem a little shocking to everybody, I accepted the offer. My new husband is a Yorkshire gentleman called Earl Sabre. He is eight years older than I am and until now a bachelor. His father died recently, so we are come north to take over the small mill he bequeathed.

'The house is quite large and situated in a bleak, lonely district. However I have the company of my husband's two maiden aunts, Miss Sarah and Miss Dorothy Sabre, both of whom are much taken with the babes. Patrick and Gobnait continue to flourish. My new husband has formally adopted them, giving them his surname, and will bring them up as his own. There is a considerable library here collected by Earl's grandfather, so I will be able to keep up my reading.

'Please convey my love and best remembrances to Dadda and the rest of the family. Mary, I suppose, has now entered the convent. I am well and much occupied with domestic duties. I hope that you are also well and did not suffer from any colds during the winter.

'I remain,
'Affectionately yours,
'Faustina Sabre.'

And that, I thought, reaching for the wax as I finished reading over the letter, would have to do. I had tried to convey the impression of security without luxury. The last thing I wanted was to make my life so attractive that one of my family would take it into their heads to visit. If they did then the aunts would learn of my previous marriage and there would be awkward questions asked about the resemblance between Sabre and the children I had borne while I was still married to Charles

O'Hara.

As I sealed the letter I realised with a little pang, that I had cut myself off from my family completely by marrying Sabre. I would never be able to return with the children as I had once thought of doing. Neither would it be easy for me ever to go down to London again for a reunion with Madame or the Pettifers. The Fausty O'Hara whose husband had died in such strange circumstances was gone for ever.

Although it was May, the wind was still bitter, the hills snowcapped. I tugged on my thick cloak and hood and changed my shoes for the calf-length boots that Sabre had bought me. I would, I decided, walk down to the village and meet the postboy who came once a month to collect any letters and deliver others that had been written. I had not yet walked the mile down to the valley, though Sabre had driven me in the trap to the counting house at the mill. I had been introduced to Thomas Leigh, a thick-set, burly man in his mid-thirties who looked like a farmer but was the clerk, and to Jeremy Watkins who was the overseer. I would have liked to go into the weaving shed and look at the great looms on which Sabre cloth was made, and meet some of the people who worked there, but when I expressed the wish to Sabre he looked amused.

'Darling, the mistress of Sabre Hall is not expected to go into the sheds. They would

189

think you most eccentric!'

I had not pressed the matter. Later on, I promised myself, I would find out more about the business from which Sabre derived his profits, but there was no sense in rushing. I was learning to curb my natural impetuosity, to think before I spoke, not to hurry heedlessly into a situation that might prove difficult.

Life had settled itself into a pattern but it was a pattern in which I had no real part. Maggie Ackroyd had taken complete charge of the babies, and when she was not nursing them or bathing them Aunt Sassie was playing with them, her rosy face tender. The twins were flourishing, so I could scarcely complain, but I wished they needed me more. There was nothing much for me to do in the household either. Huldah did the cooking and Mary did most of the cleaning, though Aunt Sassie liked to do a little dusting. Remembering all the times I had grumbled about having to prepare a meal for Chas, I couldn't help smiling at myself, but the difference was that I hadn't loved Chas, and I did love Sabre.

I loved Sabre and he loved me. Our nights together were magnificent, with no danger of our being disturbed by the crying of the babes, In his arms I could forget the brooding presence of past generations that hung over the house. And he felt exactly the same.

'This mausoleum is almost bearable now that you are here, Fausty darling. Can you wonder that I spent so much time in London before?'

'You'll be off there again when you grow weary of me,' I teased.

'How could I grow weary of the loveliest wife and the prettiest babes in the world?' he demanded. 'I want to share in their growing, not to be a stern, remote father as mine was. Do you know that, as a child, I was terrified of him? When I came home from school there was always the summons to the library where I was interrogated on every item of my school report. I used to dread that. I only set my face against the mill because he was so keen that I should take an interest.'

'And you didn't marry me until after he was dead,' I said, a trifle unwisely for the grey eyes gazing into mine were suddenly cold.

Then he laughed, pulling me close to him again. 'I married you when it was possible to do so,' he said, 'Did you really think, after Chas died, that I would allow you to take those two beautiful children out of my life? And there will be others. We will fill the house with children. That was always the trouble here when I was young. There were no other children in the family. It's a terrible thing to be an only child, with a father and two aunts, not that I don't adore Aunt Sassie, but Aunt Dotty can be a sore trial.'

'She's been very kind to me,' I objected.

'You haven't seen her when she's having one

of her spells,' he said gloomily. 'I was never allowed to bring friends home, lest she took one of her dislikes to them. She was jilted when she was a girl, you know, and she's been odd ever since.'

I would have asked more about Aunt Dotty but Sabre was kissing me again and my body arched to meet him. I thought hazily, as we sank into our deep embrace, that even if I quarrelled with Sabre my body would betray me whenever he came near.

Now, taking the letter I had written, I came out into the long gallery and walked briskly towards the stairs, consciously lifting my chin higher as I passed the portrait. I could hear Maggie singing to the babies in the nursery and a gentle snoring came from the direction of the aunts' rooms where the two ladies were taking their afternoon nap.

I went down the staircase into the hall and Mary, who was polishing the floor, jumped up to open the front door. She was a willing little thing, eager and scrawny, but so shy that I never managed to get more than a couple of words out of her.

I paused as I went through the door to enquire if she wanted me to bring anything from the village but she ducked her head, twisting her hands in her apron and murmuring that she needed nought. I left her to her polishing and was halfway across the grass when Oldfield stumped up. Apart from a small boy, who blacked the grates and slept under a table somewhere in the kitchen region, Oldfield was the sole handyman we employed. He was nearer eighty than seventy and in a perpetual ill-humour. He certainly made no secret of his dislike of me, though whether he disapproved of my being Irish or my having married Sabre wasn't clear.

'Gig's not hitched,' he announced.

'I don't need a gig. I'm walking down to the village,' I said.

'Master Sabre's at t'mill,' Oldfield said.

'I know: I'm going down to post a letter,' I said, and wondered why on earth I found it necessary to explain my actions to the servants.

'Ladies don't walk,' Oldfield said flatly.

'This one does.' I answered with equal firmness, and walked off, leaving him muttering.

Despite the cold wind I found the exercise invigorating. In recent weeks I had spent too much time indoors and it was good to be out, the icy breeze whipping colour into my face, the grass springing up again after I passed over it. In Ireland everybody walked everywhere unless they were taking a rare jaunt to Dublin, but in London I had got out of the habit.

I had gone some distance when I heard the trotting of hooves and turned, half-expecting to see Sabre. He rode down to the mill after breakfast and stayed until after dusk but he frequently came home during the day to snatch a bite and peep at the twins. It was not Sabre however but a stranger, dressed like a gentleman, save for the red-spotted neckerchief tied around his throat. From a distance he looked handsome, but, when he cantered up and drew rein at my side, I saw that he was in his fifties, brown face lined, black hair liberally peppered with grey.

'It's Mrs Sabre, isn't it? Young Earl's wife?' he enquired.

'Yes, Mr—?' I hestitated.

'Jack Gideon, ma'am,' he said. 'You'll not have heard of me but I've a farm over at Batley Tor.'

He pointed with his whip to a cluster of rocks on the horizon.

'You must be our nearest neighbour then,' I said.

'In terms of distance,' he nodded, 'but I'm not on visiting terms.'

'Oh?' I made the word into a question, but he shook his head slightly as if he refused to satisfy my curiosity and said, 'First time I've had the chance to pay my respects. Rumour has it that you're Irish.'

'Rumour has it right,' I said.

'And your accent confirms it.' He swung a leg over and dismounted his grey horse. On the ground he was shorter than he had appeared to be on horseback, but he was powerfully built, his shoulders wide, his wrists thick. There was nothing about him that attracted me, but I recognised and privately acknowledged the man's animal magnetism.

'Your own accent is not of Yorkshire, at least not entirely,' I countered.

'My mother was Yorkshire,' he said. 'My father was a Romany—gypsy, you'd say.'

'We have tinkers in Ireland,' I began, but he shook his head.

'Romanies and tinkers are not the same. When I was a lad I went on the road every summer with my dad, and then when winter came we returned to the farm to keep my mother company. After he died, I settled down to farm my land.'

'Is your mother still alive?' I enquired.

He had looped the reins of his mount over his thickly muscled forearm and had fallen into step beside me, adjusting his stride to my own.

'She died years back,' he said. 'She was never well after my dad went. They spent all their summers apart but they were closer than any other couple I ever knew. Now, tell me, how do you like it here at Sabre Hall?'

'Very well.'

'Is that really true?' He shot me a sharp glance from beneath heavy brows. 'You were married secretly, I heard.'

'In March—March last year,' I amended smoothly. 'His father would not have approved.'

'The Sabres approve of nothing they did not themselves invent,' Jack Gideon said wryly.

195

'You've children already, I hear?'

'Twins,' I said. 'Patrick and Gobnait.'

'Good Irish names,' he grinned. 'The old man would have had a fit!'

'He's dead,' I said coolly. 'The twins are mine and Sabre's.'

'Spoken with spirit!'

I was not sure if his tone mocked or approved, but his entire manner was too familiar for a new acquaintance. My own tone grew even colder as I said, 'I am settling down very well, Mr Gideon. It's kind of you to be concerned.'

'Call me Jack,' he said, unabashed by my hauteur. 'Do you have a Christian name or did you come into the world as Mrs Sabre?'

'Faustina,' I said unwillingly.

'I shall call you Mrs Fausty,' he said. 'It has a pleasant domestic ring.'

'If you are not on visiting terms,' I said, 'it is unlikely you will be calling me anything. I take it there was a quarrel?'

'You may take it as you please,' he said. 'I vowed years ago never to cross the threshold of Sabre Hall again and I'm a man of my word. However, if you ever need a friend or a word of advice in season, Jack Gideon's your man and Batley Tor's where you come.'

I am not sure what I would have answered, for he turned from me, remounting with considerable lightness for one of his bulk, and raising his hand in farewell as he wheeled around and trotted away across the moor.

I continued my walk, resolving to ask Sabre about our neighbour. There was a pony and trap, piled high with sheepskins, crossing the hump-backed bridge and I paused to let it go by. Up on the fells the shepherds were shearing their flocks of their heavy winter coats. From the open doors of the cottages came the whirring of the spinning wheels. The women spun in their own homes and the wool was then taken to the weaving shed where the looms clattered from early morning until dusk.

As I walked along the cobbled street I couldn't help contrasting the scene with what I was used to in Ireland. This street was cleaner than the ones I knew, with the refuse piled tidily on the midden behind the end cottage and not a pig in sight, but the main difference lay in the absence of children. At home there were always barefoot children, tumbling in the mud, smaller ones riding on the shoulders of older brothers and sisters, laughter and chatter filling the air. Here there was only the occasional fretful wail of a very young babe, all the children over the age of three being at work.

At the end of the street, before one reached the fenced yard of the mill, was the tiny shop with its window of bulging glass. Here, so Sabre had explained, one could obtain sugar, ginger, salt, and various remedies for the ailments that affected the villagers.

'Bertha Goodstall is a good-hearted soul, but her tongue clacks faster than the looms if you give her the opportunity! She's kind though. When I was a boy home from school, she always baked me a batch of almond tarts on my first day back. It took the sting out of my father's comments on my report!'

Bertha was at the door of her shop, bidding goodbye to the postboy who was already mounted up. I hurried up to him, taking the letter out of my pocket and handing it up to him.

'There's the money there for it to be franked in Leeds,' I said.

'Right, ma'am.' He put it into one of his two saddlebags, touched the peak of his braided red cap, and trotted away with a self-important air.

'Mrs Sabre, do come in! I thought it were thee! Tha's never walked from t'height of t'hill in this wind! Tha'll be fair run out o'breath!' Bertha was exclaiming.

'I wished to catch the postboy,' I explained.

'Happen tha nearly missed him then! He's off courting a lass over Hatherton Way and it's as much as he can do to be staying long enough to drop letters off, which reminds me there's one for thee! I were going t'send young Benjamin up with it, but seeing tha's here tha may as well take it now. Aye, courting a lass over Hatherton Way, with his mind fixed on that more than his job.' Bertha sniffed loudly.

'Young love! I've no patience with it!'

'You said there was a letter.'

'From Ireland. That'll be your home, won't it? Sent on from London, but got held up at Derby. It were franked two months since, so news'll be stale. Very elegant handwriting. A lady's hand, but clear.'

'If I could have it,' I broke into the flow.

'Won't tha come in for a sup of tea?' Bertha urged. 'Parlour's swept and kettle's on t'hob this very minute.'

'Thank you but no. I'll just take the letter.'

'Mr Sabre's not at mill,' she informed me. 'He rode up to Atherley, to take steps about a dog that's been worriting sheep.'

'Thank you, but I wasn't going to the mill. I'll just take my letter and stroll back.'

She looked disappointed, but either my firm tone or the fact that I was Sabre's wife prevented her from arguing further. Instead she heaved her plump, reluctant bulk into the musty interior of her shop and emerged, clutching the letter.

'Two months old it is, and been redirected,' she pointed out. 'Nice and thick. Happen there'll be plenty of news.'

'I expect there will.' I took it from her, lingered to assure her that Miss Sassie and Miss Dotty were both well, and finally succeeded in breaking away.

Halfway up the hill I succumbed to temptation and, seating myself on a large

199

boulder which marked a turn in the road, broke the seal. Mrs Flannigan's elegant script lay before me and I allowed my eyes to dwell on it with pleasure before I began to read.

'My dear Faustina,

'It is with a heavy heart that I take up my pen, not only to condone with you on the recent sad demise of your husband, but also to acquaint you with the sad news of your father's death. It occurred suddenly a week since and has shocked all of us very much. Your father had been to celebrate the birth of your two babies and was returning home rather late at night when he sustained a fall into the village pond and was, most unhappily, drowned.'

The elegant script blurred before my eyes. Despite the tactful phrasing I could guess only too clearly what had happened. I could see my father weaving his way home after a night's carousing, see him stumbling and falling. He must have hit his head as he fell else the shock of the cold water would surely have sobered him. I blinked rapidly to clear my vision and returned to my perusal of the letter.

'Your father was a few years past his half-century and died secure in the affections of his family and of his neighbours. In that you may surely take comfort. He was extremely proud of you rising in the world and his sorrow at the news of your own sad bereavement was tempered by the thought that you might now be coming home with your infants. My own

200

feelings, however, are somewhat mixed on this subject. While it would give me very great pleasure to see you again I do feel that your return might be a retrograde step in your own advancement. Bridget is managing very well indeed for a girl of seventeen, but the addition of three more people would severely strain her resources. Catherine has been taken into service as a maid by Mrs O'Donnell who lives in a handsome house on the outskirts of Dublin. We hear that Mary has settled very happily in the convent. She did not return here for the funeral owing to the distance but sent word that Masses would be said for your father's soul. Margaret has proved a great source of strength to Bridget in dealing with the younger boys, Sean and Stephen. Daniel has started work as a blacksmith's apprentice with Mr Tyrone. All of them wish to send their love and to assure you that they think of you often and remember you in their prayers.'

There was more, including a short letter from Father O'Brian and an ill-spelt note from Bridie but I didn't want to read any more. I folded the sheets of closely written paper and sat, my eyes still tear-blurred, on the boulder. So Dadda was gone and with him a large part of my childhood. Dadda, with his tendency to fritter away his spare coins on the winning of a wager, with his bouts of jovial drunkenness, his fund of anecdotes and pithy sayings, would not be there to greet me if I ever went back to

201

Ireland. 'When' had become 'If' I realised, and felt dull desolation sweep over me.

The boulder on which I was sitting was hard and the wind stung my cheek. I rose and began to walk rapidly up the hill. I wanted comfort and there was the possibility that Sabre might have called in at home on his way back from Atherley. At that moment I wanted very much to feel his arms around me.

His horse was cropping the grass outside the front door and I ran in, my cloak flying behind me, and called his name, feeling for the first time as I did so that I was coming home.

There were footsteps above and his tall figure emerged from the open doorway of the stair lobby.

'Must you make such a noise?' he enquired, stopping short to gaze at me. 'The babies have only just gone to sleep. Maggie had quite a time with them. She thinks Patrick may have a touch of colic.'

'My father's dead,' I interrupted quaveringly.

'Darling, I'm sorry.' His face softened as he came towards me, putting his arm around my shoulders and leading me into the drawing-room.

'I had a letter from Mrs Flannigan,' I said miserably. 'Oh, Sabre, he died two months since but the letter was held up. Madame had redirected it from London.'

'I'll get you a tot of brandy.' He pushed me

gently into a chair and walked to the side table where decanter and glasses stood. 'How did it happen?'

'He fell into the village pond and was drowned. I think he was in his cups at the time. He frequently was.'

'Drink your brandy and try and get your breath back,' Sabre advised, putting the glass into my hand. 'May I read the letter?'

'Yes, of course. Mrs Flannigan didn't know of my remarriage, of course. I had gone down to catch the postboy with a letter and found this one waiting for me.'

'Oldfield tells me you insisted on walking.'

'Oldfield said the gig wasn't hitched. Anyway I needed a walk to blow away the cobwebs.'

'It's not customary for ladies to walk,' Sabre said.

'Oldfield made that very plain,' I said resentfully. 'At home everybody walks everywhere. I realise that's not possible in London but surely, here in the country—?'

'We shall have to resume our riding lessons,' he broke in, 'and I'll teach you how to handle the gig. But it does rather lower you in the estimation of the villagers if they see you running about like a millhand, and you rushed in here like a cyclone!'

'I wanted you. My father had died!'

'He died two months ago,' Sabre pointed out.

'But I only just learned of it today.'

'And you're naturally upset.' He glanced again over the letter. 'Are your sisters and brothers in as much want as this letter hints?'

'They're not likely to come here,' I said, 'but there certainly isn't any money.'

'I shall send them some,' he said. 'One should care for the living, the dead being beyond help, my father often used to say.'

I could imagine him saying it, and was more pleased than ever that I had never met him.

'I'll see to it at once.' He spoke briskly, patting me on the shoulder. 'You ought to go up and rest for a while. This has been a shock for you, darling.'

I didn't want to go and rest. I wanted the tears, the jests, the compassion of a wake, with the neighbours crowding in to drink the corpse's soul to heaven.

'Don't wake up the babies,' he cautioned, as I finished my brandy and rose.

'No. No, I won't.'

As I made for the door I remembered that I'd not mentioned my meeting with Jack Gideon. For some reason I decided not to tell him then, but to delay it.

CHAPTER TWELVE

'They're very forward for their age. Don't you think so, Aunt Sassie?'

Sabre was on his knees, dangling a string of bright glass beads over the cradle in which Gobnait was propped against a lace pillow. Her hands, tiny dimpled starfish, shot out to clutch the prize and she gurgled with delight.

Aunt Sassie, giving Patrick a ride on her knee, glanced over and smiled.

'The little pet is a female, that's certain,' she teased. 'Look how she craves the necklace.'

'She shall have real stones when she's of an age to wear them,' Sabre said, letting the beads go. 'Amethysts and pearls and diamonds, eh, my lovely?'

'If I were you,' I advised dryly, 'I'd wait until she stops trying to eat them.'

'The Elizabethans ate powdered pearls,' Aunt Dotty observed, pausing in the doorway to look in. 'When I learned that I fear I lost a great deal of my respect for the quality of their intelligence.'

'Dotty makes the most peculiar remarks,' Aunt Sassie said disapprovingly. 'There is no telling what she is going to come out with next.'

I liked Aunt Dotty whose madness, as far as I could tell, consisted of saying exactly what was on her mind and of a slight vagueness at times as to where she actually was and what she was doing. I liked her because she had accepted me not as Sabre's bride or the mother of his children but as myself, as a person called Fausty who spoke with an Irish accent and liked to go walking by herself.

The twins were five months old and I had been four months at Sabre Hall. It would have been a lie to say I thought of it as home but at least I thought of Ireland less as the time stretched into summer and the moors bloomed gold and purple under the July sky. Sabre had sent a generous sum of money to Mrs Flannigan to be shared out among my family, but I felt remote from them all as if with Dadda's death some cord had been severed.

Sabre and Aunt Sassie were both immersed in the babes and Aunt Dotty had wandered past on her way to the kitchens where she spent much of her day making cakes and pies that were generally uneatable because she left out some vital ingredient. Beyond the windows the sunlight danced over the moor and the river below the bridge sparkled. I went out, my going unnoticed by Sabre or his aunt, and began to stroll, as had become my custom, over the fresh green turf.

Nobody had ever troubled to make a garden at Sabre Hall, though Aunt Sassie did grow vegetables at the back of the house near the stables. If a hedge were planted flowers might be coaxed to grow, out of the wind that swept down from the heights. I had suggested it but Sabre had only laughed, holding me tightly as he said.

'Darling, the soil's too thin for flowers and the only seeds you should be interested in are the ones I plant in you! There ought to be a brother or a sister for the twins before too long.'

'It's early days,' I began, but he shook his head.

'You're not feeding the babies, so there's no reason why you shouldn't conceive again within the year. Don't you want a house full of children?'

'Yes, of course,' I said, and drew his head down to mine, trying not to wonder if that was the reason why he insisted that Maggie Ackroyd should be wet nurse. His lonely childhood had bred in him such a craving for a large family that I sometimes had to remind myself that he had met and loved me first.

I had walked further than I realised and the house was diminished into the distance. I turned and looked at it. When I was within its walls it overwhelmed me with its brooding presence but, seen from the grassy knoll on which I had paused, it was simply a rather ugly, gaunt building that looked out across the valley.

'Good-day, Mrs Fausty!' The voice broke into my musing and I jumped slightly as I turned to see Jack Gideon striding towards me, leading a couple of horses.

'Mr Gideon, good-day. It's a long time since we met,' I said.

'That's not my fault, but you never come where I am,' he said, sketching a bow.

'Oh?' I looked at him in surprise.

'I've been saddling up a couple of horses most afternoons in the hope that you might take a ride with me, but the walks you take always lead in the opposite direction from the one in which I'm bound,' he said.

'I haven't been avoiding you deliberately,' I said.

'Then you'll take a ride? Only a mile or two.'

'I don't ride very well,' I said. 'In fact I hardly ever ride at all.'

'Then you've come to the right man!' he exclaimed. 'I pride myself on being a fine instructor of even the most nervous novice. Come! Up with you!'

Before I could protest he had lifted me up to the saddle of the smaller horse. It was a side saddle and I clung to the pommel in panic, but the horse stood quietly, head drooping.

'If you hook your leg over thus,' Jack Gideon said, looking faintly amused, 'you'll not need to hang on so tightly with your hands. That's better. Keep your back straight and relax. Jenny is a placid creature. We'll walk a while, and then we'll try trotting.'

He mounted up himself and took the leading rein. I found that almost imperceptibly I had begun to move in time with the horse and some of my nervousness vanished.

'With practice you could be a good rider,' he said at last. 'The trouble is that too many people go in for canters and gallops before they have learned how to sit the animal properly.'

I remembered, suddenly and vividly, how I had fallen off in the park and landed at Chas O'Hara's feet. That was how it had all begun, with Sabre introducing me to his friend, urging me to marry his friend. Only when the twins had been born had Sabre's desire for me rekindled.

'Careful! Don't jerk on the reins!' Jack Gideon's voice stirred me back from the memory of what had been.

'I don't want to ride any further,' I said abruptly. 'I'll walk for a while if you don't mind.'

'As the mistress of Sabre Hall you can do whatever pleases you, surely,' he said.

There was the same mocking quality in his smile that I'd noticed before and, in sudden irritation, I pulled my skirt free of the high pommel and scrambled somewhat inelegantly to the ground.

'I didn't mean to offend you.' He had dismounted too.

'I'm not even certain I ought to be talking to

you,' I said frankly. 'You told me you were not on visiting terms at Sabre Hall.'

'And you didn't mention me to young Earl?'

'He prefers to be called Sabre!' I said sharply.

'And who can blame him after having such a name wished on him by his grandfather?' Jack Gideon said. 'The old man never got over never being knighted. All the Sabres have marvellously high opinion of themselves.'

'With cause! They own most of the valley.'

'But not Batley Tor. That bit of land is mine, I'll not yield it.'

There was a ruthlessness in his dark face and the knuckles of his hand whitened as his fingers tightened on the leading reins. He saw me looking at him and gave me a half-rueful grin, shrugging his wide shoulders as he said,

'One day you must come over and visit.'

'Sabre might not like it.'

'He probably wouldn't. He was brought up on the tale of my perfidy, but if you've not mentioned me—'

'There was nothing to mention,' I said.

'But you're curious?' He slanted a look at me out of his deepset eyes. 'You must be.'

'Perhaps I am.'

'The aunts, Sassie and Dotty,' he said. 'What do you think of them?'

'They've both been very kind to me,' I said defensively.

'There was a time when Dotty was hoping to

be wed,' he said.

'And was jilted. Sabre told me.' I stopped, my startled gaze flying to his face. 'You? Were you the—?'

'The man who left poor Miss Dotty high and dry at the altar,' he nodded.

'Then I'm not surprised that you are not received at Sabre Hall,' I said, 'and I'm sure I ought not to be talking to you now.'

'It's not what you think,' he said. 'The truth is that old Sabre—young Earl's grandfather—wouldn't hear of his precious daughter marrying a penniless lad with a rundown farm and a Romany for a father. Then he gave in and said very grudgingly that I could marry her on condition I handed the farm over to him. That way he'd get to own the entire valley.'

'And you chose to keep your farm. Poor Aunt Dotty.'

'I agreed,' he said, 'because at that time she meant more to me than any farm. She was a pretty girl, slender as a birch with shy, eager ways like a bird or a fawn. Oh, you see her middle-aged, but I tell you she was a lovely thing. Full of tears and laughter, both coming one after the other, with sometimes no reason for either.'

'Aunt Dotty is—not always herself,' I said.

'She's crazy,' he said flatly and the remembrance of an old sorrow flashed into his face. 'She never ought to have been promised in marriage to anyone, but her father saw a

211

chance of increasing his property and took it. He took the chance of sending her toppling right over the edge into complete insanity and the strain of marriage could have done that very easily.'

'So you jilted her.'

'Left her without explanation. Her father, forgetting that he had originally opposed the match and furious at not obtaining the land, forbade me the house. That was thirty years back.'

'And you've never married?' I said curiously.

'You think I've nursed a broken heart for all that time?' He threw back his greying head and uttered a laugh that savoured more of bitterness than humour. 'No, I've never married, but I've not spent all my time in grieving for poor Dotty. I've only seen her at a distance in years. But I've cherished a fine grudge against the Sabres.'

'The old man's dead now!'

'His spirit isn't,' Jack Gideon said. 'It lived on in his son and it lives on in his grandson. They use people, Mrs Fausty, and I'd not want to see you hurt!'

'I don't think my feelings are any of your business,' I said, 'and I don't think I ought to be here listening to all this!'

'Probably not,' he said.

'Then why tell me?' I asked crossly.

'Because you married Earl Sabre and he's sufficiently like his grandfather to cause you a lot of grief.'

'That isn't true!' Colour flamed into my face. 'I've seen portraits of his grandfather and his father, and they're not in the least like him. Oh, I'll grant you there's a resemblance in colouring and features, but they look grim and ruthless.'

'Give him fifteen or twenty more years.'

'And Sabre is happy. We're both happy.'

'Then why do you walk alone on the moor?' Jack Gideon interrupted.

'Sabre has the mill to oversee,' I said, 'and he likes to spend as much time as possible with the children. That shows he's different from his father. Sabre was sent to school when he was a child and he was always afraid of his father. He is absolutely determined that his children will have only happy memories of their childhood.'

'And his wife? Does he intend her to have happy memories too?'

'Of course I'll have them,' I said coldly. 'Everybody has been most kind to me and the children are lovely. Sabre is very proud of them!'

'If you were my wife,' Jack Gideon said slowly, 'I would be so proud of you there would be little left for any children.'

'That's because you don't have any. Sabre adores the twins and he wants many more children!'

'And you?'

'Of course,' I said. 'I want a large family too.'

There was too much defiance in my voice and, a moment later, I was shocked to hear myself saying, 'I'm from a big family and our cabin was always noisy and crowded. There was never any space at home, no place in which to be private. I wanted to get away, to make something of myself.'

'And you married Earl Sabre in secret.'

'His father would have disowned him,' I said quickly.

'I don't doubt it,' Jack Gideon said, 'but I'd have thought more of young Earl if he'd had the courage to bring his bride home.'

It was on the tip of my tongue to protest that Sabre couldn't have brought me home while his father lived for at that time I was married to Chas, but as that couldn't be revealed I said icily, 'You must not presume to speak ill of my husband to me.'

'My, but we have come a long way from that Irish cabin!' he said, and put his hand on my arm, his voice changing as I started to move indignantly away, 'Ah, Mrs Fausty, don't be too quick to take offence! I'm near fifty years old and at my age I cannot learn how to stop speaking my mind. You might need a good friend one day, so it's not wise to quarrel with me.'

'I have Sabre and the aunts,' I said stubbornly.

'And your own family too,' he pointed out. 'Or have you risen so high in the world that they've fallen out of sight?'

'My parents are dead,' I told him. 'My sister, Bridie, looks after the rest. She was always a capable girl. Daniel is apprenticed to a blacksmith and Cathy's gone into service. Mary is in a convent—she always wanted to be a nun. Peg and the twins are still young and at home.'

'That's a formidable tribe,' he said feelingly.

'Tribe is right!' I exclaimed and I was suddenly telling him all about them, chattering as I had not chatted for months. I told him about Peg's hoydenish tree-climbing and of the twins playing truant to go fishing, and of Mrs Flannigan who was so anxious to see her pupils well-educated, and of the time Dadda had won five pounds on a horse and spent it all on sweetmeats and lace though the rates needed paying. As I talked they became real to me again and the cord I had believed broken tugged at my heart.

'And when Dadda died,' I finished, 'I was so disappointed not to have been at his wake. At home we are not ashamed to mourn our dead openly.'

'And a wake at Sabre Hall would not be out of place,' he nodded. 'Everything is done there as if dying were in slightly bad taste. It is because they are educated, I suppose.'

'But you are educated yourself,' I pointed

215

out.

'I picked up some along the way,' he grinned at me, 'though I never had the advantage of college. My farm's no more than a couple of miles off, so if ever you wish to drop in for a dish of tea—?'

'Thank you, but I don't think that it would be proper, under the circumstances,' I said, and couldn't help hearing how impossibly prim I sounded.

'As you please.' He gave me his lazy, mocking grin. 'Shall we ride back the rest of the way?'

'I'll walk. Thank you for the lesson.' I put out my hand politely and he took it between both of his own calloused palms, his expression changing.

'You'll make a good rider, Mrs Fausty, and I meant what I said when I offered to be your friend. I'd not want to see you hurt.'

He swung himself up to the saddle with the ease of one accustomed more to riding than walking and trotted away, the other horse following. A strange man, I thought, but he had some justification for his bitterness if the tale he'd told me was true. Sabre's grandfather must have been a dreadful man to risk his daughter's sanity for the sake of a farm. I shook off the disquiet of the thought and quickened my step. Yet there was no real reason for me to hurry. My absence, I knew, was not likely to have been noticed at all.

I didn't see Jack Gideon again for several weeks and then it was only a fleeting glimpse of him, riding past the end of the village street when I'd gone down to the shop in the gig with Aunt Sassie. It was not often that Aunt Sassie left the house and she was greeted by Bertha Goodstall as if she were exiled royalty returning. I had written a second letter to them at home, but there was no post for me, and I was reduced to trailing in Aunt Sassie's wake as she made a kind of royal progress round the closely packed shelves of the musty little shop.

It was curious, I thought, how Aunt Sassie, for all her plump cosiness, was able to dominate the place where she was. At home it was to Aunt Sassie that the servants turned for orders and Sabre for advice, and now it was Aunt Sassie who was being regaled with all the latest village gossip while I stood, unregarded.

'And I told her, Miss Sabre, that if he had not talked of wedding her then there was no point in ordering stuff for t'cake, but there! some lassies will not be told sense! There's candied violets in. You've always had a fancy for them.'

'I shall take a quarter, and a little oil of cloves, Patrick's gums are giving him a little trouble,' Aunt Sassie said.

'How are the little bairns?' Bertha enquired, tipping candied flowers into a scoop.

'Growing faster than I can measure. Patrick

217

sits up alone and is crawling quite unaided. Gobnait is the quieter of the two, but very advanced for her age. She has such a wise expression on her little face sometimes as if she understood every word said to her.'

'Maggie Ackroyd'll be fond of them,' Bertha commented, 'especially with losing her own.'

'Maggie is a treasure. We shall miss her when she goes,' Aunt Sassie agreed.

I had forgotten that Maggie's husband would soon be returning from Leeds. He would naturally want to see more of his wife and, though it was too soon for the twins to be weaned, his return would mean that she would inevitably spend less time with them. It was only now that I could begin to admit to myself that I was a little jealous of Maggie Ackroyd.

At supper that evening, the four of us seated round the massive table under the quelling stare of the portrait, I brought up the subject.

'Maggie leaving?' Sabre paused in the act of carving the roast and looked across at me in surprise. 'What put that notion into your head?'

'I didn't mean that she would be leaving at once,' I said hastily, 'but the babies won't need a wet nurse for ever, and Maggie's husband is coming back.'

'Maggie knows where her duty lies. She won't leave until the babies are weaned,' Aunt Sassie said reassuringly.

'But when she goes,' I began, but Sabre broke in.

'Huldah and Aunt Sassie will manage between them. They brought me up with fair success, I think.'

'But your mother was dead,' I pointed out, 'Patrick and Gobnait have a mother.'

'And a very lovely one.' He passed the plate to me with a slight bow.

'The point is,' I said, feeling irritation rise up in me, 'that I am capable of looking after the twins myself. As it is I scarcely ever get the opportunity even to nurse them. They will grow up without knowing me properly.'

'You will very likely have another babe to fuss over before very long,' Sabre said.

'Dear Fausty, does that mean—?' Aunt Sassie began, her pink face breaking into a smile.

'It doesn't mean anything,' I said crossly. 'I'm not talking of any future children I might have, but of the ones I have now, and I never get the chance to take care of them!'

'What Fausty means,' said Aunt Sassie, 'is that she considers I interfere.'

'Aunt, she means no such thing,' Sabre said.

'Oh, she does, she does.' The smile had turned to a crumpled look of distress, 'I have felt for some time that my poor little efforts have not met with quite the degree of appreciation for which one might hope. Not that I am complaining, my dear Fausty—

believe me, I am the last to complain. And I do understand that you don't want a foolish old woman to take your place in caring for the twins, but it was never my intention to usurp the place of mother—oh dear! I tried very hard to lift some of the burdens from your shoulders, and I have only succeeded in making you hate me!'

'Aunt Sassie, that's not true!' I protested.

'Oh, but it is.' She shook her curly grey head sorrowfully and dabbed at her eyes with a lace-edged handkerchief. 'I am not entirely insensitive to the atmosphere engendered here, and I do sense—oh, you are right, my dear. In future I won't go near the children unless you give me your permission, though it will be very hard to be denied the care of those precious ones.'

'Fausty meant nothing of the sort.' Sabre had laid down the knife and spoke with decision. 'She is absolutely delighted to have you to help with the babies.'

'I know when I am not wanted,' Aunt Sassie said faintly.

Her small eyes glittered with tears and her hand shook.

'Aunt Sassie, you mustn't upset yourself,' Sabre said. 'Fausty, tell her that you didn't mean to hurt her.'

'I didn't mean to hurt you, Aunt Sassie,' I said obediently. 'It was only I wanted more time with—of course you must spend as much time with them as you wish.'

'My lovely wife must have time in which to learn to be mistress of Sabre Hall,' Sabre said, smiling at me. 'She doesn't understand that over here it is not customary for ladies to take sole charge of their children.'

'If you'll excuse me,' I said, tightly polite, 'I'll leave the rest of the meal. I'm not really very hungry.'

'You're quite sure you're not—?' Sabre's grey eyes were hopeful.

'I'm not pregnant!' I said loudly, crumpling my napkin into a ball and dropping it on the table as I rose. 'When I find out I'm pregnant again, I do promise you that you will be the first one to know, Sabre.'

'You won't wake the babies, will you, dear?' Aunt Sassie murmured. 'Maggie will just have got them off to sleep and it's so tiring for her if they're disturbed.'

'I won't go near them,' I said, fighting down my rage. 'I wouldn't dream of ruining Maggie's efforts.'

I resisted the tempation to bang the door and went out quietly into the hall, where I stood for a moment, fists clenched, before striding across to the drawing-room. There was brandy in the decanter and I poured some for myself and gulped it down. The fiery liquid did absolutely nothing to cool my rage and in sudden exasperation I kicked savagely at Aunt Sassie's embroidery frame and sent it toppling over into the hearth.

'That's a silly thing to do,' Aunt Dotty said, opening the door and coming in. 'Much better to kick Sassie.'

'It's Sabre I'd really like to boot in a tender spot!' I said. 'He doesn't treat me as a wife at all, merely as someone who happens to have borne his children!'

'All the Sabre men treat their women that way,' Aunt Dotty said calmly, stooping to right the frame. 'You don't see any portraits of them hanging up anywhere, do you? My father worshipped land. So did my brother. Sabre wants children because he can recapture the childhood he never had through them. Poor old Sassie probably wants them too, but she never married, so it's too late to have her own. She reared Sabre after his mother died.'

'She'll not rear mine!' I interrupted fiercely.

'So you'll set yourself up against Sassie, will you?' Aunt Dotty gave me a look I can only describe as pitying. 'I warn you, fighting Sassie is like fighting a wet sponge. You'll be the one ends up soaked.'

'You only say that because nobody ever tried,' I began.

'Oh, didn't they though?' Aunt Dotty seated herself in a chair, stretching her long legs before her. 'When we were girls I tried every way I know to outwit my loving sister. I told you my father didn't want me to wed.'

'Because of your health,' I said delicately.

'Because I was crazy,' Aunt Dotty contradicted. 'As a child I had fits. The physician said I'd outgrow them and I did. Even my father couldn't pretend that I wasn't well enough to take a husband. Oh, he tried to prevent my marriage all the same. Father wasn't one to provide a dowry without an argument. Not that his giving way did me any good! I was jilted in the end. I often think Jack—his name was Jack—had heard some rumour or other and if that's so it was Sassie who'd let the cat out of the bag!'

'Yet you've gone on living with her all these years!' I exclaimed.

'Oh, Sassie will get her due deserts one day,' Aunt Dotty said, with one of her abrupt barks of laughter. 'But don't go thinking you can fight her openly. She'll drown you in her tears and smother you in those smiles she flings around. And Sabre thinks that the sun shines out of her, so if you set yourself up against Sassie you'll be setting yourself up against him too.'

'Aunt Dotty,' I said impulsively, 'if you want my opinion I don't think you're the least little bit crazy. I think you're one of the sanest people I ever met.'

'I am but mad nor-nor-west, but I can tell a hawk from a handsaw,' she said.

'I beg your pardon?'

'I was quoting, child. Shakespeare. A very fine dramatist though you, being of the poor

223

benighted Irish, will never have read him. You should. He'd a saying for every occasion.'

'What does it mean?' I enquired.

'The quotation?' Aunt Dotty gave another of her disconcerting barks of laughter and rose, looking for a fleeting instant like the bright, brown-skinned girl she must once have been.

'It means that I am—only crazy when I wish to be, and that's a very great advantage!'

CHAPTER THIRTEEN

My conversation with Aunt Dotty had cheered me immensely, making me feel that I had an ally. The situation didn't change but I had begun, outwardly at least, to accept it. Maggie Ackroyd's husband had decided to stay in Leeds for a further six months which gave ample time for the babes to be weaned and for Maggie to move back into her own cottage. There was no way in which I could complain of Maggie without exposing my own jealousy for the twins were thriving on her milk and she was clearly devoted to them. Indeed the only danger was that the babies would be ruined by too much loving for neither of them was allowed to cry for more than a minute and they had always been rocked to sleep instead of being laid down in their cradles. Aunt Sassie

made a point of hastily putting the babies
down if I came unexpectedly into the room,
and she went out of her way, whenever Sabre
was present, to enquire what dresses they
ought to wear and if it was wise to give Patrick
a drop of laudanum for the pain of his teeth.
The scene at the dining-table was not referred
to or repeated, and Sabre, putting his arms
about me as we lay in bed, murmured, 'I'm so
pleased that you and Aunt Sassie are getting
along well together. She was a young woman
when my own mother died and she sacrificed
any chance of marriage in order to bring me
up. That's why we must have a large family, my
darling, to carry on the family name.'

'And provide Aunt Sassie with lots of babies
she can nurse,' I said.

He missed the dryness in my voice and
merely kissed me, saying he was glad I'd come
to realise how devoted Aunt Sassie was to the
children and how much her help relieved me
of effort.

I kissed him back, wiser now than to argue
with him, but something in me marvelled at his
blindness. I loved Sabre still. His handsome
face and figure, his charm and generosity, were
as potent as when I had first seen him, but I
was beginning to know him better now. There
was a weakness in him, bred of his lonely
childhood, and there was nothing I could do to
make him realise the fact.

At least it was full summer. I had not

realised before how beautiful the moors would look when they were all carpeted in gorse and heather, nor how the delicate harebells would blow a lavender mist against the grey rocks that bestrode the horizon. There were star-shaped blossoms on the thorn bushes and bluebells nodded at their reflections in the rushing river. I took long walks, each time penetrating deeper into the surrounding countryside, learning the folds and crevices of the landscape and beginning to love them with almost as much passion as I had once loved the gentler hills of Ireland.

Nobody complained any more about my unladylike passion for exercise. I suspected it was because my absences left the field clear for Aunt Sassie to spend as much time with the babies as possible. I made up my mind that when winter confined me within the gray walls of Sabre Hall I would think of some way to remedy matters but meanwhile I was glad to be out in the sunshine and the wind, which had a sharp edge even in August and whipped colour into my cheeks.

August became September and only the fading of the heather told me that October was almost here, for the days were still long and light. I must have walked further than I realised one particular day towards the end of the month for, when I rounded a corner between two jagged crests of heather clad rock, I saw ahead of me a modest farmhouse, set snugly in a walled yard. As I stood looking at it, a big rough-haired dog scampered out, barking at me in a manner that savoured more of welcome than of threat.

'Rufus! Here, boy!' The voice was unmistakable and I was suprised by the leap of pleasure I felt as Jack Gideon came striding towards me.

'Mrs Fausty, so you decided to come and drink tea with me at last!' he exclaimed. 'Or were you hoping for another riding lesson?'

'I didn't know this was your farm,' I said, feeling absurdly shy as I met his mocking gaze.

'Then you probably didn't notice when I pointed out the general direction,' he said, his eyes still laughing at me. 'Now that you are here you can't refuse to come in.'

'I'm not sure.' I hesitated.

'I hardly think that there's any cause for scandal in the visit of a respectably married lady to a neighbour old enough to be her father,' he said.

'For ten minutes then.' I fell into step beside him and we walked together down the path to where a barred gate interrupted the stone wall. At the other side a few hens scratched and clucked contentedly in the dirt and from the pigsty a sow grunted.

'It's more like Ireland than anything I've seen here yet!' I said, enchanted.

'We don't all earn our living from Sabre Mill,' he told me. 'This place is largely self-sufficient. I sell my fleece over in York.'

'Why?' I enquired.

'Because it doesn't please me to put profit in Sabre pockets,' he said bluntly. 'Mind your head. The lintel is low and you're a tall woman.'

'Too tall,' I said ruefully as I ducked into a large chamber that ran from back to front of the house. 'I always wanted to be dainty.'

'Nonsense! You're the right height for your build. Sit down and I'll mash the tea.'

I took one of the big railed chairs that stood at each side of the hearth, and looked about me. The room was large and low-ceilinged, the sunlight slanting through the tiny window-panes. There were sheepskin rugs on the floor and a faded patchwork cover had been thrown over the high-backed settle. A round table was laid with a checked cloth and Jack Gideon lifted down two earthenware mugs from a shelf against the wall.

'Kettle's on the hob,' he said cheerfully.

'Thank you. This is a lovely room,' I said appreciatively.

'Not as fine as the ones at Sabre Hall.'

'But more friendly,' I said and blushed, aware that whenever I met Jack Gideon I seemed to say more than I intended.

'I keep the house in good order for an old bachelor, I think,' he said easily.

'Aunt Dotty would have been happy here,' I said.

'If marriage hadn't sent her right out of her mind. I couldn't take the risk.'

He poured boiling water into a large teapot and stirred the contents with a long-handled spoon.

'Who told you of her condition?' I asked.

'You can be sure it wasn't her father,' he answered grimly. 'Once old Sabre was convinced that I was set on marrying her he was too eager to get his hands on Batley Tor to be anxious for me to know the truth. No, it was Sassie who plucked up the courage to tell me. I never cared much for Sassie, but I admired her that day. She was the only one who had the kindness to let me know.'

'You had no idea?' I queried.

'Oh, there were vague rumours,' he said. 'I knew she'd had funny spells when she was a child, but I never realised—hell, Mrs Fausty, we were both young and who's to say we'd have ever really suited?'

'You never got the chance to find out, did you?' I muttered, accepting the mug of blackish tea he was handing to me.

'Ah, well, it was a long time ago, and poor Dotty's certainly proved a mite eccentric in the years since,' he said easily.

I wanted to argue that for some people it was easier to slip into craziness than to live with a broken heart, but it was too late for both of them now. Aunt Sassie, I thought, had done her work well.

'We'll not waste time on old tales,' he said abruptly, moving his heavy shoulders as if he eased some burden resting on them. 'Tell me about yourself. You look in fine fettle but your words tell me a different story. Is that husband of yours neglecting you?'

'No, of course not!' I said indignantly. 'We are both very happy together, I promise you! And the twins are well and growing fast.'

'There would be something very wrong with them if they weren't growing,' he said, and I found myself laughing with him in a way I had not laughed for months.

'Mrs Fausty, I'm sure your twins are the most beautiful and the most advanced children in Yorkshire,' he said at last, 'but you really cannot expect a mere male to take a consuming interest in a couple of squalling infants! Tell me about yourself. Have you had word from your family?'

'Only that they are well.'

'And why haven't you come for a riding lesson?' he demanded. 'I told you that you had some potential as a horsewoman if you persevered.'

'I prefer my own legs and feet, thank you,' I retorted crisply.

'And nobody grumbles at you for behaving like a hoyden?'

'Nobody notices much where I go or what I do,' I said, despising myself for the forlorn note that had crept into my voice.

'Drink up your tea,' he said. 'Then I'll show you the rest of the house. My mother stitched the linen herself, years ago when she spent the long summer months waiting for my father to come home from his travelling, and he carved most of the furniture when he was at home during the winters.'

'And they were happy, you said?'

'Happy as larks. Can't you feel the echo of it within these walls?'

I could, though it was an impression that was hard to define in words. I knew only that there was a feeling of warmth in this large, homely room that was missing at Sabre Hall.

'I'm sorry that you never married,' I said.

'Oh, Rufus and I get along together well enough, don't we, boy?' He glanced across at the big dog who thumped a plumy tail on the floor.

'And I must go. I'll see the rest of the house on another occasion,' I said, putting down my cup and rising to shake off the curious spell that wove around me.

'So there is to be another occasion? I'm delighted to hear it,' he said, rising too. His eyes mocked me again and the intimacy that had sprung up between us vanished. When he opened the door I went through hurriedly, without looking back.

'I'll walk with you a spell,' he offered, but I shook my head.

'Sabre will be home soon. He spends most

days at the mill, you know.'

'A most worthy employer. His father would be proud of him.'

'He takes a close interest in what will be his children's inheritance,' I said tartly. 'His father had nothing to do with it.'

'He should find time to take his wife walking,' Jack Gideon said. 'One day he'll turn round and find—'

'Find what?' I asked abruptly, for he had paused.

'Find you drinking tea with another man,' he finished.

'Mr Gideon, what is it you want of me?' I asked, stopping to face him. 'I may be young but I'm not a fool. You went out of your way to make my acquaintance even though you have not been received at Sabre Hall for years, and you know that I'll not talk about my meetings with you.'

'Why not?' he enquired lazily, bending to unlatch the gate.

'It would embarrass Aunt Dotty,' I said uncomfortably. 'And Sabre might not approve.'

'And you naturally wish to please your husband.'

'I love my husband. We married for love.'

'Secretly, lest his father disinherit him,' he nodded.

'What do you want?' I repeated. 'Are you hoping to renew your friendship with Aunt Dotty? She really is not as mad as people think. Sometimes I think she is not mad at all really—only pretending to be.'

'I got over my passion for Dotty years ago,' he interrupted impatiently. 'Oh, I still hold a grudge against the Sabres. First they considered me too low to wed into their precious family and then they—old Sabre, I mean—would have taken my farm and married me to a sick girl with no regard either for us or for any children we might have.'

'You said you were not interested in children.'

'I dare say I'd be interested in my own, even if I wouldn't be as besotted as young Earl appears to be with the twins.'

'You haven't answered my question,' I said.

'As to why I seek your friendship?' He shot me an amused look from his deepset eyes. 'Mrs Fausty, when you go back to Sabre Hall promise me that you'll go straight to your glass and take a long look at yourself. You're nearly thirty years younger than I am but when you laugh I feel like a boy again. Isn't that reason enough for me to seek your company?'

'It's not a good reason,' I said faintly. 'You can't recapture your lost youth in my company. That would be—wrong.'

'What wrong can there be in an innocent friendship?' he countered.

But there was nothing innocent in the expression on his dark face as he stared at me, and there was no friendship in the way his hand reached out to tug the shawl from my head and tangle in my hair.

I jerked aside sharply, the colour rushing into my cheeks.

'I frightened you,' he said, dropping his hand at once. 'I spoke too soon, before you were ready.'

'Ready for what? For you? Mother of God, but what put that into your mind?'

'You yourself, pretty Mrs Fausty,' he said. 'You're a lovely, lovely woman.'

'And a married one!'

'Married to a man who spends his time at work and allows his wife to seek company elsewhere! You deserve more than that.'

'I do beg you,' I said, trying to hem the ragged edges of my dignity, 'not to say anything else. You have made it impossible now for us to be friends. I shall never come here again!'

'When you're weary of wandering alone,' Jack Gideon said, the mockery back in his voice and eyes, 'you'll return to me, and I will give you more pleasure than Sabre ever could.'

I broke away from him and started to walk rapidly away, too proud to run though I felt sick and shamed, and all my liking for him had vanished. He had betrayed the trust I had begun to repose in him, and I could forgive neither of us for that.

He had made no attempt to follow me but I went on walking fast, my heart thumping, the palms of my hands wet with sweat. Dear God, but the man must be crazy, I reflected, slowing my steps at last when I was out of sight of the farm. Either crazy or he had some scheme in his mind which involved me.

I stopped, catching my breath as a stitch tortured my side, pulling my shawl over my disordered hair. If I arrived back in such a state even Aunt Sassie would guess that something had happened. I was not even sure myself exactly what had happened, save that Jack Gideon had turned and shown me his other face. And, for a brief moment, something in me had been tempted.

I began to hurry again, resolving that in future I would stay near the house and the village and avoid Batley Tor. Whatever Jack Gideon's intentions I was determined to frustrate them. I had begun to like him. Perhaps some part of me had known in which direction I was walking and hoped to see him. If that was true then I was in more danger than I realised.

For the first time the walls of Sabre Hall were a welcome refuge. I went in and ran up the stairs to our big bedchamber where I could compose myself before facing the rest of the family.

'There you are, Fausty! Everybody wondered where you'd gone.'

Sabre must have come home early from the mill. He was adjusting his cravat before the mirror and the glance he turned upon me was mildly impatient.

'I'm sorry. I went for a walk.' I spoke jerkily, conscious that my face was scarlet and that, having done nothing wrong, I felt absurdly guilty.

'You spend too much time alone,' he said. 'Aunt Sassie frets that you might be homesick. She was saying that next year you might like to take a trip to Dublin.'

For a moment anticipation leapt in me. Then I said, 'Would you come with me, Sabre?'

'Darling, one of us ought to stay with the children.'

'We could leave them with Aunt Sassie.'

'And I wouldn't care to spend too much time away from the mill. I neglected my duty so much when I ought to have been learning the business that I need to catch up now.'

'And you don't want to leave the babies,' I said.

'Isn't it natural for a father to want to spend time with his children?'

His tone was reasonable, his eyes loving as they rested on me, but I was chilled. He looked at me as the mother of all his future children, as if I were not really a person in my own right at all. If there were no more children he would cease to look at me at all and then I might be tempted to turn to the dark faced man at Batley Tor.

I found myself taking off my shawl, moving towards him, slipping my arms about his neck, the spark that had been kindled in me on the moor rising into flame as I whispered,

'Don't let's go downstairs yet. There is no hurry. No hurry!'

CHAPTER FOURTEEN

It was a golden October that year. I have only to close my eyes to see it again in its glory, with the gorse spreading its blanket of beauty over the hills and the hills themselves merging to the horizon in tints of blue, lavender and purple. The small harvest from our two wheatfields at the other side of the valley had been gathered into the big barn and our sheep still roamed the heights, cropping the short tender grass. Only in the early mornings, when a grey mist obscured the landscape, did the approach of winter enter my mind.

'Winters are harsh here,' Sabre said. 'The roads are often deep in drifts and some of the remote farmsteads are snowed in. If it doesn't snow it rains and that's almost worse. The valleys flood and the animals have to be moved to higher ground.'

'We shall be comfortable enough here,' I said lazily.

'Will you, Fausty?' He raised himself to look

down into my face. 'Are you really contented here?'

It was so rare for him to enquire into the state of my feelings that I gaped at him for a moment before countering with, 'Why shouldn't we?'

'Aunt Sassie feels you haven't really settled here.'

'Aunt Sassie!' I made some impatient movement and he said, 'Aunt Sassie is very fond of you. She wants you to be happy here.'

'I am happy,' I said.

'When the winter's over I shall send you to Ireland for a visit, or down to London. Wouldn't you like to see your friends there again?'

'The Pettifers and Madame. They were neighbours, not really friends. Anyway, I don't think I shall be paying any visits anywhere for at least a year.'

'Are you sick? You don't look sick.' He peered at me more closely, a frown on his face.

'I'm not sick,' I said, and laughed in sudden delight, unable to keep my suspicion to myself any longer. 'I'm pregnant.'

'Are you certain?' His frown deepened for a moment.

'As certain as I can be at such an early stage, but it will be next summer before the child is born. Are you pleased?'

'Pleased?' He looked down at me and I saw the frown vanish. 'Oh, Fausty, if you only knew

238

how pleased! I've hoped for months that you'd quicken again soon. Oh, Fausty, I love you now more than I ever thought possible!'

I said nothing as his lips pressed mine but some of my pleasure had diminished. It was natural for a man to feel a particular tenderness for his wife when she was with child, but Sabre was too transparent in his joy. I wanted him to say that he would love me for the rest of our lives even if I never bore another child, but his kiss was one of gratitude, not passion.

'You must take care of youself, my darling,' he was saying. 'No more tramping across the moors. If the mist came down suddenly—and it often does at this time of the year—you might easily be lost or fall and injure the baby.'

'And myself,' I said reproachfully.

'And yourself,' he agreed, and kissed me again very lightly. 'We cannot risk harm to either of you, sweetheart. Between us we'll found a dynasty, eh? The Sabre dynasty.'

'A dynasty,' I echoed, but when I would have kissed him with more warmth he drew away, regret in his face.

'We cannot risk any lovemaking now until after the baby is born. You ought to rest, my sweet.'

I didn't want to rest. Although I had been sick very early that morning I was now full of energy. I could have made love for hours and danced afterwards but Sabre was rising, tucking the quilt about me, moving across to where his garments were hung over the back of the chair.

'I'm riding down to the mill,' he said, 'to go over the accounts with Leigh, but I'll be home soon. We'll celebrate this evening. I'll tell Huldah to make something special for supper and we'll open a bottle of champagne. Father laid down a good wine cellar—I'll say that for him!'

Watching him as he dressed I was swept by a regretful tenderness. He had never known a happy childhood and so, rather than accept the fact and find a greater fulfilment in his marriage, he sought to experience what he had missed through his children. He was eight years older than me, but I felt immeasurably older than he was as I lay and watched him dress.

When he had gone, I rose and put on my own garments, aware of my own body as I had not been aware of it for some time. The tell-tale signs of pregnancy were already apparent in the darkening of the skin round my nipples and the faint rounding of my hips. Soon my belly would swell and I would have to exchange my narrow-skirted gowns for loose-fitting dresses that would disguise my misshapen figure. Whatever charms Jack Gideon had found in me would have vanished, I thought, and then was annoyed with myself for thinking of the wretched man at all. I had not seen him since I had fled from his advances at the farm and I was determined never to meet him again.

Dressed, my hair drawn back in a style I hope made me look more adult and less girlish, I went down the gallery to the babies' room. They were both awake, sitting like small monarchs against their plump pillows. Two pairs of Sabre grey eyes turned in my direction and Maggie, who was tidying the room, dropped a curtsey as I entered.

'I were just getting stuff ready for t'wash,' she said.

'Take it down to Huldah and then have a walk,' I said on impulse.

'Walk where, ma'am?' she enquired.

'Anywhere. It doesn't matter where you walk,' I said impatiently, 'as long as you get a little exercise and fresh air.'

'I'm not supposed to leave t'bairns,' she began doubtfully. 'Miss Sassie said—'

'I'm here now,' I broke in firmly. 'I can amuse the children. After all I won't always have you to depend on. When you go home—'

'But didn't Miss Sassie tell thee?' she interrupted.

'Tell me what?'

'She's asked me to stay on as nursemaid and my man'll be handyman here, soon as he gets back from Leeds. Oldfield's getting past t'heavy labour and there's need for another man. Miss Sassie said as t'were all fixed up.'

241

'Did she indeed?'

'It's all right, ma'am? There's naught wrong?' she asked anxiously.

'Nothing's wrong.' I spoke gently for it was not, after all, her fault. 'Go down with the washing and then take your walk.'

'Yes, ma'am.' She gave me a faintly puzzled look as she withdrew and Gobnait, sensing a familiar figure was leaving her orbit, screwed up her tiny face in preparation for a yell.

'Hush now, alanna!' I pulled back the covers and reached for my daughter, bouncing her small, firm body up and down on my knee as I crooned to her in the Gaelic I'd not used for months. The look of misery changed to a delighted gurgle as she tried to pull herself to a standing position and from his cradle Patrick gave an excited yell.

'My dear Fausty, what in heaven's name do you think you're doing?' Aunt Sassie, grey curls bristling with indignation, came through the door.

'Playing with the twins,' I said coolly.

'Over-exciting them, more like!' She almost snatched the baby from me and stared at me reproachfully over the top of the small red head. 'Gobnait will bring up her feed if you jiggle her like that. Where's Maggie Ackroyd?'

'I sent her for a walk.'

'We don't employ her to take walks,' Aunt Sassie said.

'*You* don't employ her at all! It's Sabre who

242

engages the servants and pays their wages. Maggie says you've asked her to stay on.'

'She and her husband are both good workers. There'll be no need for them to live in. Huldah and I can manage at night.'

'I'll be looking after the babes myself,' I said tightly, 'as soon as they're weaned.'

'But you won't be able to, will you?' she said, glancing at me as she settled Gobnait back in the cradle. 'Sabre just told me the happy news.'

'It's not certain yet.'

'Oh, I think it must be, dear, else you'd not have risked raising Sabre's hopes,' she murmured. 'You'll have your hands full with the new baby, no time to spare for Patrick or Gobnait, and when the new babe is born you'll be paying a long visit to your relatives in Ireland. You can feel free to stay as long as you please without fretting about the children. The twins will be safe in my care and we'll be able to find a healthy wet nurse for the new little one.'

'And you will remain as virtual mistress of Sabre Hall, I suppose?'

'It's my home, dear Fausty,' she said mildly. 'Isn't it natural that I should want to stay, that I should want to help Sabre and give him the benefit of my experienced advice?'

'I'm not going on any visit to Ireland!' I flared. 'I'll not stay here to become a kind of child-bearing cipher either! I'm Sabre's wife and a wife is a mistress of her husband's house!'

'Was it like that with your first husband, dear?' she enquired.

'What?'

'Your first husband, Charles O'Hara. He came to a most untimely end, didn't he? Oh, I haven't told Sabre what I know. I haven't told anyone at all. You really didn't imagine that I wouldn't make some enquiries about the bride my nephew had chosen, did you? It was convenient for you, wasn't it, to have your husband die just after you'd given birth to Sabre's children.'

'It was an accident. The inquest—'

'I was fortunate enough to obtain an account of the proceedings,' she interrupted. 'It made most interesting reading. You were wise to give out that you'd been married secretly.'

'The twins were legally adopted.'

'And Patrick will inherit Sabre Hall, as he should. It will be a great pleasure to rear him, as I reared Sabre, as I would have reared my own if I had ever married.'

'You ought to have married,' I said harshly. 'You ought to have had a family of your own!'

'Nobody ever offered for me,' she said. 'I was very pretty and I wanted to be wed, but my father discouraged suitors. I was the elder and it was my duty to take care of poor Dotty. She used to have fits, you see, and the physician

244

had warned that only the bearing of a babe might stabilise her.'

'But she was not able to marry! I thought that—'

'The physician who examined her confided in me.' Aunt Sassie said. 'He left the district soon afterwards, so I—perhaps I did get his words a trifle muddled.'

'And told Jack Gideon that marriage would make her completely insane.'

'I might have done. The physician could have been mistaken and I was too fond of Dotty to let her take the risk.' Her pink face was sulky and she burst out with an almost childish pique. 'She wasn't as pretty as I was but she had a suitor! It wasn't fair that she should marry and I should remain spinster!'

'So you made yourself mistress here instead!' I stopped, my ears catching some faint sound in the gallery beyond the half-open door but I heard nothing save the rattling of the seeds as Patrick shook his rattle impatiently.

'I have devoted myself to Sabre,' Aunt Sassie said. 'I won't allow an upstart Irish woman, with a dubious past, to spoil that.'

'You cannot stop it,' I said, and a new energy bubbled up in me as if the coming child gave me strength. 'I don't want my children to know the truth about their birth. Naturally I don't, because it would hurt and embarrass them. And I don't believe you would make

245

anything public either, because it would hurt Sabre also. If you fling mud at me you fling it at him too!'

'After the new baby is born,' she said with a frightening sweetness in her expression, 'you will go to Ireland, my dear. If you do not I may be forced to tell Sabre about your clandestine meetings with Jack Gideon.'

'That's a lie,' I said, but the words came out on a gasp and I could feel the colour ebbing from my face.

'No, dear Fausty!' Small and plump, she rounded on me triumphantly. 'Oldfield saw you meet Jack Gideon on the moor, and you were seen again quite recently hurrying away from Batley Tor.'

'Accidental, innocent encounters.'

'But you never mentioned them to Sabre, did you? He'd have told me if you had.'

'When I learned who Jack Gideon was,' I said gaspingly, 'I thought it wiser to say nothing for fear of bringing back painful memories.'

'And soon after Oldfield saw you coming from Batley Tor you announced that you were with child.' Aunt Sassie laughed softly. 'I do hope, for your sake, the new baby has red hair!'

'There is nothing—Jack Gideon is old!'

'He'll be about forty-seven years old by now,' she said. 'When he decided not to marry Dotty, because of the risk to her health, he told me that he'd never forgive my father for being willing to sacrifice his daughter for the sake of a little extra land. He swore he'd be even one day, and your coming must have made him very hopeful. What better way to get even than to cuckold his enemy's grandson?'

'He didn't seduce me,' I said, dry-mouthed.

'I wonder if Sabre would believe that,' she murmured. 'Of course, if you leave everything as it is, if you spend most of your time between babies in your native Dublin, I see no reason at all why he should ever know, do you?'

There was a red mist before my eyes and I wanted quite simply to kill her. I wanted to smash my clenched fist into the middle of that round, amiable face with its tiny eyes and aureole of grey curls. Aunt Sassie had won. Whatever she chose to tell Sabre, whatever twisted tale she invented, he would believe her, just as Jack Gideon had believed her. It would have been some comfort to be able to believe that it was Aunt Sassie who was the crazy one, but it was obvious she was coldly, frighteningly sane.

'I'll go down and tell Maggie to come back,' Aunt Sassie's voice said out of the red mist that surrounded her. 'You ought to rest dear, rest is most important in the early stages, I believe. I'll have Huldah bring you up a nice cup of coffee.'

She went out and the mist cleared, leaving me in a grey desolation. The palms of my hands hurt where I had dug my nails into them and I drew my breath in great, shuddering gulps. I was beaten and there was nothing I could do. I wondered if Sabre's mother had ever felt as I did now, if she too had ever tried to fight against Aunt Sassie's gentle ruthlessness, if in the end she had not minded dying.

'Is everything all right, ma'am?' I blinked as Maggie's voice roused me from the stupor in which I sat.

'Yes, of course. It's merely that I-I don't feel very well,' I said numbly.

'Miss Dotty neither,' Maggie said. 'She came down a few minutes since, white as chalk, and came rushing past me like she'd seen the Shuck hound of death!'

'Going where?' I asked sharply.

'Down to the barn, I think. I did start after her but Miss Sassie said she'd go and see what was up. Can I get on with my work now?'

'Yes. Yes, of course,' I said, rising on shaky legs.

'Best lie down if tha's not well,' Maggie said.

'I think I will.' Somehow I got out of the room and made my way back to the bedchamber. My bedchamber, which I would occupy by courtesy of Aunt Sassie, until she chose to drive me out altogether. There was nothing I could do, nothing but wait. I remembered the soft sound I thought I heard out in the gallery. If Aunt Dotty had been there, listening to some part of the conversation—? I sat down on the edge of the bed, resting my head on my hands, conscious of the slow ticking of the clock as the time crawled past.

There was a tap on the door and I raised my head, realising that I must have been sitting in the same position for longer than I had thought for my hands were cramped and I felt dizzy.

'It's only me, dear.' Aunt Dotty came into the room, wiping her hand down the side of her skirt. She sounded slightly breathless, as if she had been running, and there were wisps of straw in her untidy hair, but she seemed calm.

'Aunt Dotty.' I pushed back my hair. 'Are you all right?'

'Yes. Yes, my dear. Perfectly all right now, and so pleased about the child. Sabre told me on his way out to the mill. He has wanted another child for a long time.'

'For Aunt Sassie to rear,' I said.

'Sassie always wanted to be married,' Aunt Dotty said, sitting next to me and patting my hand. 'I suppose that was why she lied to Jack. I often wondered why he jilted me, but I always thought it was my father who told him I was a little crazy, I never did blame Jack, you know. Perhaps it would never have worked— our marriage, I mean.'

'You heard. Aunt Dotty, I'm so sorry.'

'I was in the gallery coming up to tell you

how pleased I was at the news of your baby. I heard her accuse you of some terrible things and I heard her gloat over the way she lied to Jack Gideon. She was always cruel unless one was a child. She loved children, you know, sometimes I think she would have liked Sabre to have remained a child. My brother was always harsh with him, you know. He took after our father.'

'She will take this child too,' I heard myself say. 'She will drive me back to Ireland and turn Sabre against me, and there's nothing I can do!'

'Now you really mustn't get into a fret.' She patted my hand again. 'Sometimes, you know, I feel quite sorry for people who are not crazy. They are so much less able to cope with anxiety! Sassie was a very ill-intentioned person, even when she was a girl.'

'Aunt Dotty, why do you keep saying "was"?' I asked, turning my head to look at her. 'She's not likely to change, is she? I shall have to go back to Ireland save for brief visits here so that I can get pregnant again, and Sabre will accept it! She will work on him until he does accept it.'

'You worry too much,' said Aunt Dotty calmly. There was something in that calmness that rang warning bells along my nerves. I rose, staring down at her, hearing from below a sudden commotion of voices and footseps.

'Aunt Dotty, where is Aunt Sassie?' I heard

myself ask. 'She followed you out to the barn, Maggie said. Where is she?'

'Perhaps she got accidentally locked in,' Aunt Dotty murmured. 'There are pears stored in the loft above and the ladder's very rickety. Oldfield should have done something about it months ago, but he's getting on—'

I whisked across the room and down the wide gallery to the stairs. From below I could hear Huldah, her voice raised high in fearful excitement, and I picked up my skirts and ran the rest of the way down the stairs, into the stone-flagged hall where the front door stood wide. Huldah caught me by the arm but I shook her off, running out on to the sloping grass. Away to the left smoke and flames billowed up into the October sky, and from the valley tiny figures scurried like ants.

'They had no chance, Mrs Fausty.' It was Huldah who spoke, hands tangling in her apron. 'The roof caved in when he went to drag her out.'

'He?' My mouth was dry and my eyes burned as if they had been scorched by the flames.

'Mr Sabre was riding back from t'mill and Miss Sassie—we saw her at t'barn window, flame all round her, and he went in and roof caved over them both! Oh, Mrs Fausty, he were that devoted to her! She reared him from a child!'

EPILOGUE

1819

They were buried in adjoining graves, and a year later the two headstones were firmly fixed in place, the lettering an elegant gold.

HERE LIE THE REMAINS
OF
SARAH SABRE
BORN 1771 DIED 1818
REST IN PEACE
HERE LIE THE REMAINS
OF
EARL SABRE
BORN 1792 DIED 1818
HE GAVE HIS LIFE FOR ANOTHER

And that was true, I thought. Aunt Sassie had sucked him dry of his independence just as his father had drained him of courage. My beautiful Sabre had been no more than a handsome shell, seeking to find his own identity in his children and never really loving me at all. He had used me as the vessel in which to beget more babies just as I had used Charles O'Hara to stand father for my bastards. There was a certain ironic justice in that.

The inquest had been simple and the verdict unquestioned, largely due to Aunt Dotty who had given her evidence in a calm, rational manner.

'I was in the barn when my sister came in. I'd run down there to get some pears from the loft but Sassie said she'd collect them and so I went back to the house. The loft was dim but there was a lantern and Sassie must have kindled it. The ladder was not safe. We even remarked on the fact when we were in the barn and Sassie said she would bring it to Oldfield's attention. She must have fallen on her way down, the lantern flying from her hand to ignite the straw. Perhaps she was dazed by the fall or the door jammed. It did sometimes jam.'

Sabre must have seen her frantically banging on the tiny window, as he rode back to the house, and burst in to rescue her. Much would remain speculation but it was agreed that aunt and nephew had been devoted and that Sabre had given his life to save her. Great sympathy was felt for me and it was deemed a miracle that, after the traditional months of seclusion, I had given birth to healthy twin girls.

I looked at them now as they slept peacefully in their cradles in what had been Aunt Sassie's bedchamber. Both had red hair, though Fanny's was of a lighter shade than Esther's. They were placid babies and I was feeding them myself.

'You might marry again. You're still very young,' Aunt Dotty had said.

I shook my head. I would never love any man as I had loved Sabre and I had sufficient money to be independent now.

'I'll run the mill,' I said crisply. 'I don't know anything about the business for Sabre never told me and he only took me there once, but I'll learn. I'll learn it from the bottom up, Aunt Dotty, and I'll keep the profits high! By the time Patrick takes over I'll have something worth showing!'

It was odd to realise that my lively, toddling son now owned mill and hall, but the interest on the capital was mine for the rest of my life and Sabre's will had provided a separate sum to be divided equally among any other children he might have had. My three little girls would all have dowries.

The lawyer had explained it to me and I sat demure in my black gown, my mass of curly hair pinned into a matronly knot, and listened gravely.

Of Jack Gideon I had seen and heard nothing. I never wanted to set eyes on him again. I was finished with flawed men who used me only for their own ends.

I left the sleeping babies and went into the gallery. From one of the long windows I could see Aunt Dotty romping with Patrick and Gobnait on the grass below. When spring came I would plant a hedge and make a garden behind it, sheltered from the moorland wind.

Someone was watching me. I spun round and caught the painted gaze of Sabre's grandfather. For a moment a pang shivered through me for the eyes were those of the only man I had loved and then I lifted the heavy portrait from the wall and put my heel through it, grinding the old canvas into fragments. I would have my own portrait painted to hang there instead, I decided. Faustina Sabre, Mistress of Sabre Hall. True founder of a dynasty.

We hope you have enjoyed this Large Print book. Other Chivers Press or Thorndike Press Large Print books are available at your library or directly from the publishers.

For more information about current and forthcoming titles, please call or write, without obligation, to:

Chivers Press Limited
Windsor Bridge Road
Bath BA2 3AX
England
Tel. (01225) 335336

OR

Thorndike Press
P.O. Box 159
Thorndike, Maine 04986
USA
Tel. (800) 223-2336

All our Large Print titles are designed for easy reading, and all our books are made to last.